A RED ROSE

Written By

A.J. Guzwin

This author has also written 2 fairy stories, about a heroine called 'Dark Rose', over 750 poems, and a Shakespeare-style tragic drama. He also provides some illustrations.

A.J. Guzwin

ISBN: 979-8-89397-018-0

Table of Contents

Chapter 1

THE PALACE OF DARKNESS

A windswept bay looking out on a menacing dark storm-studded horizon....

Suddenly, from the shallow nearer waves, a seaweed-haired, rather blue-faced apparition emerged, spluttered … then spoke.

"Where the heck are we?"

From the struggling flotsam, another youthful shape arose, looked around, and mumbled, "Hector, old chap, I haven't a clue." He shook himself vigorously, then added, "Our ship was scheduled to arrive at Hobart in about two hours, and we were hit by a very strong northeaster; so, I'm guessing we're somewhere in South Australia."

A third damp youth was washed ashore, along with two cubs – the one a lion, the other a bear, and last to reach land was a small, very soggy rabbit.

Through a shimmer of salt water that was still stinging their eyes, there now appeared something extraordinary. Over the grass dunes at the top of the beach walked, very purposefully, a large black monkey wearing what looked like a magician's cloak – deep blue satin with sparkles which, as he got nearer, were seen to be small gold stars, moons and planets.

"Ahem!" coughed the Monkey. "Would you care to come to my place for a warm bath, a change of clothes, and a bite to eat?"

"Wow! Sure!" cried the lion, who rarely refused the chance of any free food. "That's OK, isn't it, Keeper?" He spoke to the slightly freckled, tufty-haired geography 'expert.'

"If that magic monk is on the level, it's very kind of him, and we're all desperately in need of a meal, but keep your eyes open," replied Keeper, lowering his voice for the last comment, as hoping that he would not offend their prospective host. He then smiled at the monkey and said, "Thank you. That is extremely kind."

After trudging through a patch of scrubland, they spotted a prominent hill in the near distance, surrounded by a quite thick dark mist. The Monkey led the still damp and sorry-looking strangers along a half-overgrown stony track ever closer to the mist, increasingly similar to a black thundercloud, within which loomed, even darker, a spire-turreted neo-gothic edifice.

"Looks as though we're going to get soaked again," muttered Hector.

"I don't like mouthy little squirts," said the lion, glancing down at the rabbit.

"And I'm not too keen on bone-headed, muscle-bound show-offs," quipped the rabbit, quickly and instinctively dodging towards the protection of the fair-complexioned, curly-haired blond lad.

"Bunny, will you stop provoking Jim!" He addressed the smaller animal while manually fending off the other.

"From here on," said Monkey when they were almost alongside a black, standing rock and about two hundred metres from the sinister arched Gothic entrance, "you must, one behind another, follow my footsteps precisely, because there is only one safe route through my booby traps."

"Booby traps…." A mighty whisper came from Bunny. "Why not a nice pathway, lots of flowers, and a normal stretch of lawn?"

Monkey explained patiently: "I'm afraid we have enemies not far away, and defensive measures are really necessary."

Despite the light-hearted comment, the poor rabbit was on the verge of hysterics.

"Hey, Targah, he really does look for*lorn*!" Jim punned, trying to cheer the bunny with a dreadful joke.

Targah, the third youth, did not answer but promptly lifted up the rabbit and then carefully stepped onwards, mimicking Monkey's every movement.

"Isn't Targah brave!" said Keeper as he encouraged the little bear to follow.

"Or stupid – like me:" the lion cub grinned and softly padded behind them.

"Concentrate," ordered Monkey, "or your life-span will be very short."

To everyone's relief, they entered the Palace of Darkness, as their host called it, without any casualties.

"Who are the enemies you spoke of?" asked Hector.

Monkey answered quietly, "Witches and wizards. Some came from Europe when they knew they weren't wanted, but the weirder ones are said to be from the planet Pluto.

"On a more positive note, the nearby town, Barleybag, is a friendly place. Several businesses there, including a chain of garages, a rather daunting private medical service, and a wholesale cut rubies outlet, are run by our local Branston-style entrepreneur and ultra-capitalist whom you will get to know simply as 'Ducky. 'He lives in a cavern (about two miles outside the town), which holds his ruby mine and is guarded by a multi-headed snaky monster that he calls 'chief of the serpents'."

It was a weird new experience to partake of Monkey's hospitality. A ghostly gong sounded along an arched corridor, and they entered a hexagonal room boasting a magnificent circular, brightly variegated, and somewhat Turkish-looking chandelier.

"Do sit down and relax," said their host.

"?" thought Jim… "But there aren't any chairs!

Monkey, as if guessing the dilemma, gracefully indicated the carpet and sat there, picnic-style, then clapped his hands together in an authoritative way.

Bunny yelped as two wraith-like light green shapes glided forward: the foremost had a moustached and bearded face, tight green and yellow cap, large round earrings, and three gold necklaces, each of a different length. What started as head, chest and arms became, when one glanced down, a narrow column of greenish, half-luminous smoke. He also carried what looked like a slim firework, that is, a wand from which sparks flew like a demented gas lighter.

"Supper, please, for the assembled guests and myself," ordered Monkey.

A vivid green flash was directed at one of the six walls. A hidden doorway appeared, and a long table slid out, containing a veritable feast.

"Wow!" said Ted. Bunny and Keeper just stared; Hector's eyebrows rose; Targah looked dumbfounded.

"It's a buffet," explained Monkey, "so stretch or starve."

The young lion was first to fill his plate and glass, trying everything – a Bitter Banana, mango pop, tropical cheesecake, and so on: in fact, he enjoyed it all, except for Monkey's own favourite drink, a foul-tasting bright green juice.

"Um… upside down pudding," said Targah. "Is that to welcome us to Australia?"

Hector groaned.

"Talking of welcome, I'm considering a sort of housewarming party here," said Monkey. "I haven't really had more than one or two guests since living here… and the place does look rather menacing from the outside."

"Isn't this place warm enough?" asked Jim, who was now full of calories and sitting on a radiator.

"Some of it is scary on the inside," whispered Bunny to Ted, thinking of genies and booby traps.

"Some female company would no doubt be appreciated," Monkey continued.

Targah's eyes lit up, and he nodded.

"But no painted squaws!" muttered Hector.

"Nor ghastly, very dumb blondes," added Keeper emphatically.

Monkey smiled. "I think you can trust my judgment."

He appeared to have already determined the guest list.

Chapter 2

MISS LANGTON

"September the Fifth… Hey!" thought Keeper. "Today is to be Monkey's housewarming party. I'd better smarten up."

He half slid, half rolled out of bed. Dozily, like a seasick drunken crab, he staggered to the exquisite washroom, already crowded by his two brothers – Hector spraying aftershave everywhere and Targah combing his enviably thick blond hair assiduously. Then he spotted Jim, who elaborated an explanation: "They've been told that some highly eligible young ladies will be present this evening."

"Now he tells me!" Keeper's mind raced savagely.

After what seemed an interminable delay, the room at the sink became free, and he tidied his ragged, unruly parting and brushed his teeth vigorously, inwardly thanking Monkey for providing them all needed toiletries, even some spicy cologne. Finally, a glance at the mirror suggested reasonably smart presentability, and with a dark grey suit, pastel blue shirt, and a sky-blue tartan patterned tie, Keeper raced to join the others in the main hall.

Various exotic buffet salads lined the side walls. Neon-bright balloons, holly, eucalyptus fronds, and multi-colored mini-lights festooned the window arches.

There was a teenage version of Monkey, consequently to be introduced and known as "Baby" – manning the impressive lantern-lit foyer and announcing the visiting company as they arrived.

"Mr. Chuck Rogers… Lady Sheila McCubbin… Miss Amy Boolagong… "

Gradually, the room became a sea of sound and colour. Keeper glanced at the small orchestra occupying a large window bay. It was a mix of simian and human players. A funky gibbon with a bow tie and silk waistcoat was playing clarinet next to an elegantly dressed lady flautist and a red-faced male saxophonist. Three fierce-looking baboons wielded trombones. With his double bass, a gorilla towered over the demure girl second violinist, who in turn flanked a darkly handsome vocalist cum-guitar-player. A capuchin played viola next to a brown-haired lady cellist. At the back, an apparently spaced-out orangutan lovingly played a myriad of arpeggios on a large golden harp.

"I wonder if some girl here will be crazy enough to want to dance – or even talk – to me?" Keeper pondered. "I am probably one of the world's ten worst dancers. But as for chat, she'll probably be less bored by me than some lugs who have a serious lack of imagination or scruples – or both."

He noticed a radiant blue-eyed blonde talking to his brother Targah. The back of Hector was visible, whirling a sandy-haired maiden towards the far latticed arches. Everywhere, there was a bustle of happy youth.

A friendly smile beamed across the room with a magnetic effect, leaving everyone and everything else in blurred shadow.

Instantly, more than a decade of memories flooded his brain – Brentwood, Gravesend, East Dean, the South Downs, Reigate, Riverside, etc…

There she stood, elegance and grandeur personified.

Dodging carefully between the dancing couples with just a few bogus dance manoeuvres, Keeper moved towards the young lady across the room. She wore a neatly fitting part-frilled white blouse, classic deep red skirt, golden stockings, and tiny crystal earrings set against her wealth of harmoniously bunched jet-black hair.

"Hello, Nature … or do you prefer I call you Samantha?" He mumbled, pausing before her -

Her face reddened with an enchanting mix of shyness, embarrassment, and welcome.

- "It's been a long time… too long. You are looking well."

"Thank you. So are you! I'm known as Nature around Oz. But what brings you here?"

"I know: it's an amazing coincidence that we should meet again so far from home."

As she gazed at him with a patient smile, Keeper realized he had not yet answered her question.

"Uh… sorry, yes: either destiny or a happy accident meant that we were washed up from a wrecked vessel onto a beach near here – just two days ago, so I haven't a clue whether the beach has a name, but our host tells us that we're in the vicinity of Barleybag, South Australia."

He would have gladly gone on talking forever as long as he was looking at her and she at him, especially as she showed absolutely no sign of getting bored, though he was also torn by the desire to find out all she might want to tell him about her life and aims.

She broke in: "Wow! The shipwreck sounds scary. Thank heaven you're safe! Your brothers are with you?"

"Yes. Hector's over there, and Targah's not far away. I'm surprised you're not dancing."

"Maybe I'm waiting for the right man to invite me."

As if on cue, there was a musical lull; then Monkey called out: "Take your partners for the Emperor Waltz."

'It's now or never,' thought Keeper –

– "Well, in case Mr. Perfect doesn't show, how about we stumble around the floor for a while?... though it's only fair to tell you I'm probably one of the world's worst dancers."

"Don't worry. I'm equally hopeless."

The thrill of holding the girl of his dreams, with his one arm really round her waist, and the other clasping such a warm, responsive hand, that, and the closeness of her fresh and lovely face, eyes smiling into his – it was too distracting for him to know how his feet were moving. Still, by some inexplicable miracle, he never once trod on her toes. Too absorbed to notice whether he had restricted the movements of more capable, real dancers, Keeper felt a reverie of unfeigned and spontaneous togetherness.

"Don't wake me up," he muttered.

"Oh, you are funny!" Nature's laugh had a musical quality. "We are supposed to sit down now," she added.

He hadn't realised that all the other music had stopped, but in a half-stupefied daze, he escorted the precious girl back to a seat near where they had begun waltzing.

"I think we just invented a new dance," suggested Nature with lowered eyelids. "… it was nice."

They sat together in a point-arched alcove.

"Tell me all about yourself," asked Keeper. "And what you've been doing."

"Alright … starting from when I particularly remember… that you were dressed very formally – in fact, much like tonight… I attended a school for young ladies but cannot boast a heap of qualifications. Nevertheless, with some help from friends and family, or sometimes all on my own, I learned how to do a few useful things like house improvement, interior design, understanding and looking after animals, and how to get a good meal together while staying healthy. People seem to like to come to me for help and counsel. I'm told I'm a good listener.

I like lazy holidays in the sun, but equally enjoy short walks by a lake or stream, through woods with lots of wild nature, and a quiet bench or smooth tree-stump where the sights and sounds of the countryside are all around."

"Your name – Nature – seems so apt… Do you still have those two little doggies, Bella and Sasha?"

"Yes. They're quite grown up now, though. We'll have to arrange for you to meet them soon."

"I'll look forward to it."

"Only … I have to go now. The family's arranged taxi will already be waiting outside. I didn't realize the time."

Nature smiled, blew a kiss, and vanished past the red velvet curtains.

After slowly recovering his wits, Keeper was suddenly hit by the sickening realization that he didn't know her address or phone number.

'A Cinderella mystery, but with no abandoned shoe,' he thought glumly.

"Excuse me." He dashed past two smartly dressed genies, reached the large oak door, and swung it open, only to see a Land Cruiser taxi disappearing fast into the distance.

Chapter 3

MISUNDERSTANDINGS AND MEMORIES

Breakfast next morning

– Jim, Bunny, and Ted had been chasing each other around the bedroom until a half-awake Hector growled: "Monkey's home, not yours; so don't wreck it! ... And tidy up those pillows and chairs."

"You still seem quite tired," said Monkey as he replaced the muesli dishes with hot mushroom and tomato toasties.

"You're right," Keeper admitted. "Miss Langton and I had a wonderful evening. I now believe I almost know how to dance."

"What?" Hector suddenly yelled. "She was with me!"

"That doesn't make sense," put in Targah slowly, "unless …"

"I will have blood!" continued Hector, brandishing the ketchup.

The young animals had barely started laying odds on the outcome when Monkey spoiled their sadistic fun by pronouncing, "Young men acting like children! Your memories of experience in Britain should have told you that there are THREE Miss Langtons. It's a straight case of three brothers teaming up with three sisters."

In the next dramatic pause, his words sunk in.

Hector put down the ketchup bottle, though he had inadvertently sprinkled from the rather loose lid enough to make Bunny look like a war-painted Red Indian.' Teamed up'?" he thought: "That sounds rather horsy."

"Wow!" said Jim. "Cupid's darts are flying everywhere! That's about as likely as winning the Lottery."

"I think there's a history to this," pondered Ted, the self-styled sleuth, "and I think it goes back to when these love-struck lads were back in England."

"Just take that mushy gloat off your faces," threatened Hector, especially glowering at Bunny, "or it may lead to painful consequences."

"If you are prepared to behave yourselves," started Keeper, "I'll clear up a few details as far as I am concerned."

"Yes, please carry on," said Ted.

"When I was younger," Keeper continued, "I knew a lovely princess who asked me just to call her Sammy…"

"Isn't that a boy's name?" objected Jim.

"It can be, if it's short for Samuel, but – like 'Sam' – it can, and here does, stand for Samantha."

"Like Chris for Christopher or Christine," put in Hector.

"Ah-hem!" coughed Keeper. "Do you want the story?"

"SSSSH!" - (noisy whisper from Bunny)

"It was right at the end of the summer holidays. Our family had traveled by train to visit people Dad knew in Lower Brentwood. I remember coming out of a long, pitch-dark tunnel suddenly to view a blue sky, a church overlooking green cliffs, and a modest station with a clump of silver birch trees. A short walk later, we reached the Langtons' home, a grey stone terraced, perhaps Edwardian house with a few steps up to the front door. With a polite welcome, we were ushered in, and then I saw this beautiful girl with very dark brown eyes and a cascade of silky jet-black hair near the top of the stairs. Yes, it was Samantha. Her smile went right through me. The older brother was weighing me up, slowly and half nervously; the younger looked careful and philosophical.

"I think we had a cheese or ham salad at the dining table, and I noticed a glass-fronted bookcase and garden window, while opposite, facing the road, was a bay-shaped window with heavy curtains. At one side of the front, sitting-room area, was a black upright piano, while at the back was a chest of drawers, having upon it some varied simple ornaments, including a sweet monochrome photo which I instantly recognised as a slightly younger Sam.

"While the older generation engaged in profound conversation, the younger ones headed through the back door. As the boys rough and tumbled on the path or grass, playing catch with apples from a kind sister, Sammy had clambered up one of the apple trees and sat, a cosy princess, surveying us from her woody balcony.

"After a while, we were told we would be off to the shops, followed by a trip to a nearby rec and lido. Targah and I were intrigued by some brightly coloured realistic Red Indian models; Sam was treated to a little brooch with an emerald-coloured centre.

"Then we walked together to the nearby park. After seeing much hilarity on the roundabout, see-saw, children's slide, and colourful swings, we quickly headed for the pastel blue changing rooms. We were soon splashing about heartily with plenty of joyful noise. There were inflatable rings, tyres for the older ones, a small water slide, one lifeguard sitting on a half-chair, half-ladder, with a whistle the size of a large firework, and getting a deep bronze sun tan. I remember Sammy wore a green, frilly costume and just screwed her eyes up as her brothers were jumping like bombs or flicking armfuls of water to drench her face, though her grimace quickly changed to a radiant smile... "

Keeper's face took on a rather dreamy look.

"Tell us more later on," interjected Jim and pulled Ted with him out into the hall, murmuring in the bear's ear, "Let him daydream. We can explore Monkey's pad now, without grown-up interference."

Ted started to follow him, then asked, "What about Bunny?"

"Oh, leave him: he likes soppy stories … and, anyway, I'd like some time away from the pesky rabbit because he enjoys winding me up."

At the end of the green-walled corridor, they entered a darkened room. On the left wall, between big velvet tied-back curtains, was a massive screen.

"I'd never guess Monkey was into computers," said Jim.

Ted studied the console below the screen.

This is more than just a computer. It includes a powerful CCTV, plus a camera obscura with about a five-mile range on a good day. It means Monkey can look out for invaders and see what's going on anywhere around here."

"Does it have a name?"

He calls it his 'Magic Mirror'."

Jim looked closely into the screen.

"Hey!" he suddenly cried. "Isn't that a witch?"

The screen had split into nine sections. One of these now became outlined in vivid red and then filled the whole display, while at the same time, a light started flashing, and a trumpet-like alarm sounded.

"Look: the text below says 'basement level, north side.' I'm going down there to sort out this intruder!"

As Jim rushed towards a nearby hexagonal lift, Ted called after him: "Be careful! And I'll try to find and warn Monkey."

The lift quickly brought Jim down to the lowest passage level. It was quite cool and a little damp, but he could see coming towards him a red witch with a black eyepatch, a large shoulder bag, but no obvious weapon. This enemy, whom he would later know as Witch Broth, reached a tennis-ball-sized eerily blue sphere from her bag and rolled it forward with a determined underarm movement as if the lion cub's legs were cricket stumps. On contact, it emitted a drowsy, pungent, smoky gas…. Jim reeled helplessly, keeled over, and then fell unconscious.

The witch's look of malignant triumph suddenly changed as various bright red and green lights flashed from the passage walls: a solid steel sheet now dropped to cut Broth off from her intended victim. Monkey knew how to cope with the intruder. His automatic alarm system brought three genies and himself to the rescue – reviving Jim with some weird, jasmine-scented smelling salts, blasting a super-powered air-conditioning salvo through a valve in the walls, and then raising the steel sheet in readiness to deal with the unwanted guest.

Broth was too canny to stay around and, with a short curse, retreated as fast as possible.

"Shall we chase?" asked one genie.

"Not this time," answered Monkey. "She might lead you into a trap, and, anyway, our priority is to bring this reckless, sorry lion cub back to friends and safety."

He gave Jim a cold, angry stare. "Learn an enemy's strengths and weaknesses before you engage in battle! Broth has a massive cauldron into- which she specializes in mixing all sorts of foul soups, liquids, and gases for hostile purposes. Take good warning!"

Chapter 4

A DAY OUT

Some while later, Keeper was happily meeting his date.

Nature looked gorgeous (when didn't she?), wearing a sandy orange, cool but figure-hugging top, and a squaw-style, medium-length, black dress with a shred-patterned hem.

Keeper drove her to a quaint mock Tudor pub near a tranquil church and right next to a small tributary of the River Murray known as the Wombat.

"How about some lunch?" he asked.

"What, here?" Nature's eyes lit up.

"First, come and look around."

Upstairs was a quiet little dining area in a neat, Old-English style, with exposed tar-black roof beams.

"Shall we eat here or outside?" he asked.

"It's such a nice day. Let's be outside," she replied.

"Yes, inside can wait until the weather changes," agreed Keeper.

At the back of the restaurant, the patio veranda, laid out with tables and chairs, was surrounded by a waist-high fence, through and over which one could watch the peaceful river winding between willows and eucalyptus.

"I fancy the seasonal salad with braised salmon," said Keeper. "How about you?"

"Yes, he fancies me too," thought Nature happily. "I'd like the same, please."

A neatly attired waitress had instructed them to order at the bar; so they obliged, giving their table number as at the corner with the best view of the trees and water for Nature and a lovely view of her for Keeper.

"What would you like to drink?" asked a hovering waiter.

To sum up, it was a lovely meal. Afterward, Keeper and Nature opted for a meadow walk.

There lay a refreshing calm on the landscape – a sea of summer green hues only bound by the very cerulean sky and, at closer range, the olive waters of the brook.

"Can you hear the crickets?" asked Nature. "My, it's so peaceful."

They walked about fifty yards.

"Let's sit down… How about here?" she added.

"I should have brought a rug or something," Keeper replied.

"Don't worry about grass stains: the ground is quite dry," she reassured him, allowing the sun to dance on her arms, legs, and back.

For a while, there were no other persons in sight. Then, a small, friendly, red-brown dog appeared, followed shortly by its master.

"Cute!" said Nature, clearly meaning the dog.

Again, there was a lull.

Then, she suddenly gasped with apprehension.

"Here's another dog – and I think it's dangerous."

A large, almost black creature with bloodshot eyes and nasty-looking teeth bounded towards them.

Keeper instinctively seized a branch from the closest thicket, breaking it over his knee. Thus armed, he moved forward and brought it down with full force towards the menacing jaws. It broke on impact as he still held it, but fortunately, about six inches of tougher consistency jammed between the hound's upper and lower teeth.

"At least it can't bite us for the moment," decided Keeper, "… but it looks really mad."

"It IS mad," whispered Nature, reading his thoughts. "Rabies, I'd guess.

"That was neatly done with the stick!"

"Actually, I was trying to hit the creature full on the nose," he confessed. "It is supposed to deter some animals."

"But not when they are in this state," she answered, and she carefully threw three tablets taken from her shoulder bag, the last one right on target inside of the dog's mouth.

Within a matter of seconds, with white froth churning around its gums, the animal turned disorientated and dizzy; then its legs gave way, and with a plaintive whine, it crumpled to the ground.

"Have you killed it?" asked Keeper, stupefied.

"Hopefully not. There is a strong chance that the ultra-potent herbal mix will simply leave him unconscious and attack the rabid condition in the brain."

He looked at her with open-mouthed wonder.

"Where and when did you learn all that?"

"Oh, I've always been fascinated by biology, especially plants, smaller animals, and botanical remedies. Maybe that was Mum's subconscious wish when I was named 'Nature.'

"By the way, I noticed how, with that branch, you stepped between me and the dog. Thank you."

"I pray that if there were no branch available, I should still be able to stand between you and danger," he said simply.

A later date prompted the following letter from the besotted youth.

Dear Nature,

It was lovely to see you today. They said the weather would be uncertain, but as I waited by the hotel's taxi-rank lamp post, you came out, and so did the sun.

Now, as I write, too far away, it is dark and raining. I live in memories till we meet again - visions of an enchanting walk. No brambles would ever want to scratch you, and blackberries defied gravity to stay in your hand. Now, though, the plums I wanted to give you are over; rose blooms that I intended for you have withered - like me - in your absence. I am counting the days, hours, minutes... living, or rather -simply existing for the moments when I can see you be with you, stay with you. Yours always, K

Chapter 5

RABBIT AND OTHER PROBLEMS

Boo, a mute psychopathic small white innocent-faced rabbit, had been warned to keep away from Spawn Grange, a dark and foreboding old mansion, mostly surrounded by swamp and frequently visited by pink-headed vultures above and venomous reptiles below.

As he passed any creature that moved, Boo bopped it into two dimensions with a swing of his long right front 'unlucky' paw.

Suddenly, the sky became a grid, and a heavy net dropped over him. He looked up into the coldest, evil, sadistic face he'd ever seen. His attempts to bop it were foiled by the meshes of the net.

"Ha, a rabbit," said Spawn, the dreadful witch on whose territory, and now courtyard, Boo had trespassed. "This should relieve boredom during lunch."

"Help!" thought Boo. "Are they going to roast and eat me?" *

No, their foul meal was already cauldron-boiled and ready. Boo was placed with a heavy foot-chain on the cold, damp slabs. Then, a large carrot was lowered on a string in front of him, but as he reached to bite some, it was hauled just out of reach. The process was repeated amidst cackles of delight from around their outdoor table.

The meal over, Spawn rose and announced, "I think it's time now to question the geologist."

"Question?" thought Boo. "I bet that means 'torture' Help!

"Hey, wait. I'm not a geologist. Hooray! It must mean someone else." Boo adopted an 'I'm all right, Jack' attitude to self-preservation.

[*What Boo was thinking can be guessed from his auto-boo-graphical notes.]

A pale, bespectacled figure appeared, flanked by two extremely burly witches.

"String him up," ordered Spawn.

The unfortunate man was quickly suspended upside down by a rope above the still-steaming hot cauldron.

"I told you that rabbit was trouble." Bunny lay in a thick clump of undergrowth near the courtyard and was whispering to a blackened-faced leaf-helmeted commando squatting nearby. "I'm glad I set O'Hare to trail him."

"Yes," admitted Keeper (the commando): "that Boo could start a war even at the South Pole."

"So let me deal with the bigger problem first." Bunny edged on all fours towards the back of the small, shackled, pinkie-white rabbit.

Suddenly, there was a loud scream from the dangling engineer.

"**Yaagh!** OK, I'll take you to the blue rocks!"

Spawn gave a snarl of triumph and bade his cronies remove their victim from above the seething pot.

"So; lead the way," he hissed.

Prodded persuasively by the vicious Spawn, the hapless engineer led them off, fortunately in almost the opposite direction from Bunny and Keeper.

By now, Bunny had reached the shackled Boo. "Oh-oh - we need a key."

The captive's mouth was making vigorous munching movements.

"What's with him?" asked Keeper, puzzled.

"Ignore it. He just wants a carrot and expects us to have brought some."

"Now we must try to help Spawn's other captive," said Keeper. "Listen and look for any clues as to where they've gone."

Ducky flew high and began to spiral outwards. Suddenly, he stopped, a tiny dot hovering almost exactly southeast.

Quietly and quickly, Keeper and Bunny moved in that direction, eyes peeled for possible booby traps or rear-guard lookouts.

"There's a bit of torn coat," whispered Keeper. "Unless it was plain luck, that engineer had the sense to brush past this thorny branch, hoping it would rip enough to clue possible rescuers."

"I can hear voices," mouthed Bunny, who'd had his one floppy ear on the ground, Red-Indian style.

"Quick – between the bushes," mouthed Keeper and led the way.

As they peered out of a particularly leafy shrub, they beheld the small group – Spawn, four other witches, and their captive – standing at a rock cleft near a waterfall.

"It's here," said the geologist, quickly adding, "but you'll need my expertise to get it all out."

"Get started then," snarled one skinny, snub-nosed witch who clearly wanted to impress his boss.

The unfortunate prisoner knelt down and pointed to a spot next to a skull and just inside the cleft.

"If I had my small spade, I'd dig there," he whimpered, "… but I'll try with my hands."

"Out of the way!" hissed Spawn, knocking him to the ground.

"Shall I kill him now?" asked the skinny witch.

"No, you moron!

He might have lied to us. Let's find the stuff first."

Using the flats of their swords, two witches scraped and scrabbled furiously at the indicated place.

Cacophonous cackles of delight split the air as they clawed out gleaming emeralds, turquoise, and marcasite.

"Now you are dispensable," said Spawn, standing over the geologist with a sadistic gloat and lifting his sword aloft.

CLUNK!

A hard and jagged small rock struck the back of the witch's neck. The sword dropped, missing the intended victim, who had instinctively rolled to the side.

As Spawn struggled groggily to maintain his balance, Keeper was there and followed up by slamming the villainous head sharply against the ravine wall. Bunny raced forward and tripped the dizzy witch leader before the others recovered from their shocked surprise so that he span downwards into the churning well of the waterfall.

"Bravo!" said Keeper as he elbowed the skinny witch, who was trying to sneak up on him with a dagger. "Right!" he shouted: "who's next?"

The three remaining witches hesitated. One grabbed a spear and advanced two steps, but then a great howl arose as the geologist, though still on all fours, grabbed the dropped dagger and spiked the witch's ankle.

"Don't move!" came a squawked command from the sky: "We've got you covered!"

A double-bed-sized heavy blanket, weighted mid-sides and on the corners, was dropped by a flotilla of large winged birds –condors at a guess, engulfing the remaining two witches instantly.

"Thanks for your timely arrival," said Bunny to their duck friend, who had now reached the ground: "Come and help me practise our Boy Scout knots on these losers."

They trussed up the defeated witches.

"Now, what do you suggest we do with them?" Ducky spoke to Keeper.

But the geologist butted in: "They nearly murdered me, and they were **so** keen to obey their bloodthirsty boss…." He continued with gritted teeth: "Let them follow their leader."

Before anyone could stop him, he shoved each bound captive into the path of the raging waterfall.

"Barbaric but understandable in the circumstances," observed Bunny with a shudder.

"Yes, I'd like to have questioned them, at least," answered Keeper.

"I only wish Spawn had been trussed up, too, before falling down there," said Ducky. "It would take a miracle for even a very strong fish to survive that … but if Spawn's lungs ever breathe again, he'll be bent on terrible revenge."

"Don't give me nightmares," said Bunny. "Let's all cheer up and head back. I've grabbed the witches' keys, so I'll get and free Boo. Come for supper at my place."

"No way!" said Ducky. "I sounded the glum note, so I'll take the rap and feast you at the Cavern. You know how to get there. I'll just fly ahead and put a few nut roasts in the oven. See you soon."

"When he said 'No way,'" commented Bunny as the duck disappeared into the sky, "I thought he didn't like my cooking."

"Your hospitality is fine," assured Keeper. "Ducky can be horribly blunt, even tactless, in his choice of words, but he really has a good heart.

Chapter 6

SPAWN'S REVENGE

"It's a grand day for a walk," commented Keeper.

He had parked his newly acquired Crusader convertible (which he nicknamed 'Sadie') in a shaded spot and was heartened at her affirmative smiling nod.

After ascending a few concrete steps from the car park, they encountered a level, neatly cut lawn area divided by a tarmac path. To the left was a colourful children's playground. Nature strode resolutely up to an empty swing, which was clearly designed for the bigger teenagers. Sitting with a dreamy sigh, she then said mischievously, "Push me!"

Keeper obliged, observing, "I'm sure you were a little tearaway on the swings since primary school."

Nature did **not** shout, "Wheeee!" but a few giggles between short, contented gasps showed that she was having fun.

"Not so high!" she pleaded: "I don't want to go right over!" He desisted. After five minutes and her equilibrium restored, they began to walk on, though Keeper paused to buy two iced coffee sorbets (with straws). The warm, hazy March afternoon sun diffused the scene as they followed the coastal path of the estuary. A few ships were visible in the variegated green, blue, and sepia water, their distant smoke puffs too lazy to rise to the apricot-edged cirrus clouds.

A shadow crossed the sky; several more followed, and it quickly grew darker. There flew down a wave of black, pointed-hat, broomstick-mounted shapes.

A yellowed, claw-like hand seized the hapless girl.

"Spawn!" Nature uttered a strangled cry.

Keeper, though unarmed, desperately flattened one witch with a left punch, pulled another off a broomstick, and chopped the back of its neck, but then he was struck from behind and fell stunned.

When he regained focus, Nature was gone. Towards the horizon was what seemed to be a fading swarm of giant gnats.

At Barleybag military HQ that evening, there was a death-like silence as the enormity of the situation sank in.

Eventually, Hector spoke: "Why do you think they didn't kill or carry off Keeper, too?

"Or instead," thought Keeper bitterly as he slumped on the large table.

"I'm guessing," Steemer spoke slowly and carefully, "that Spawn's game is to demoralize **all** of us by reducing our leader to a contagiously nervous wreck. They know that if they simply killed him, we would find another leader somehow and be fired up for revenge."

"There's another aspect," added Hector. "They may be using Nature as a bargaining counter so that they can control Keeper and, by extension, control everybody: we'd be no more than their puppets."

"Then it might be easier if I went missing," thought Keeper.

"Is there any slim chance we can plan a rescue mission?" asked Targah. "I guess they may well want to use or misuse her considerable herbal skills and knowledge."

"They'll expect us to try and may be planning a bloodthirsty ambush as a bonus," answered Steemer.

"So we send in a spy force –just one or two of us," suggested Hector.

"Good thinking, but it should not be by air. After Ducky's brilliant recent work, they'll be on full alert with ground-to-air artillery, rockets, broom patrols, aerial booby traps –anything you can think of. This time, we should use camouflaged commando methods, crawling on all fours, with wire-cutters, mine detectors, heavy-duty wet suits, or whatever else may be needed."

"From the aerial reconnaissance, we know there is a nasty-looking marsh, swamp, whatever, surrounding the area. There must be some way through – a secret path or two… unless they only move by broomsticks or tunnels."

"Yes, for how else could they move any large equipment if necessary?"

"I should warn you," put in Ducky, "That on that scouting flight, I nearly choked to death from the foul marsh stench that rises there."

"So who should be sent to spy the ground and, if possible, locate where they're holding Nature?"

Hector quickly added, "Several of us would volunteer, but who would be best for the job?"

"I'm going," said Keeper shortly.

"But… "

Steemer and Hector exchanged glances, and Targah seemed worried.

"They'll expect you, and your heart is understandably ruling your head," advised Hector.

"I guess there'll be guards and patrols after dark," said Steemer. "I suggest setting off after lunch. Foul weather would be useful, but we can't control that."

His advice made good sense. The mongrel dog known as Scruffy, who was of brown mud colour anyway and seemed the least upset - even strangely pleased – at Ducky's vivid description of the putrid marsh area, now pulled on a camouflaged helmet and was raring to go.

"It's **just** camouflage," Keeper pointed out: "it won't make you invisible… but I'm really grateful that you're willing to risk your neck." His voice choked as he smiled at the brave animal.

The dog sensed the affection and loudly demanded, "**HUGS!**" and proceeded to almost strangle his leader.

Keeper wrenched himself free and sternly addressed the impudent pup: "If you make that row on assignment, we'll both be dead ducks."

"Choose your words more carefully, please," asked Ducky.

Hector laughed, then clapped Keeper on the back. "Best of luck! If they start shooting, don't forget to **du**… I mean, hit the dirt."

"Lovely!" said Scruffy.

Chapter 7

LOSS OF A LEADER

A quick lunch took place.

Then Hector presented each of the daring duo with a small travel flask.

"This stuff's quite potent," he explained. "Make sure to drink it all before you cross the swamp; then, you won't be so bothered by the stench there."

Steemer glanced across and nodded.

It was time to move. They set off – the determined youth and a jaunty dog.

About half an hour later, Keeper whispered, "There's a smell like rotten eggs. We must be almost at the start of the swamp."

"Time for our drinks," reminded Scruffy.

"Well done – but not so loud!" hissed Keeper. "Cheers!" he whispered, then drained his flask.

Suddenly, his knees gave way, and he blacked out.

"OK, Scruffy," said Hector's voice from the deep grass behind him. "If you still feel up to it, off you go!"

Turning to Steemer, who lay nearby, he commented, "That drug worked a treat. He's out like a light."

They quietly advanced: Hector lifted Keeper's body onto his back while Steemer kept watch.

Scruffy's small but plump shape was squelching like a moving blob through the marsh.

"How can he abide that stink?" wondered Steemer aloud.

"Beats me. He appears to love anything pongy or messy," replied Hector with a shrug, "but this venture could bring us some vital information. I hope he's successful and fast, in case Keeper comes round and rushes stupidly into danger."

"Don't worry about that score. I want you to lock your comatose brother in the guardhouse, at least until that doggie returns."

A long, tense wait followed.

"It's been nearly two hours," muttered Steemer, "but I guess that's how long it would take."

Hector took a swig of tonic. "Faugh! I can smell that marsh even in this drink!"

"No – it's me."

Hector turned to see the proudly pungent, muck-covered little monster.

"Ugh! Have a quick bath," said Steemer, half choking.

"But being a spy is dirty work!" declared the shameless mutt, who hated getting washed.

Steemer had anticipated this and, though groggy, signalled to Targah, who was now quietly hovering in the doorway with a big bucket of very soapy water.

"Ouch! Geroff! Talk about gratitude!" The canine hero was thoroughly drenched.

After laughing at the grumpy dog, the two youths walked through to the small, high-fenced lawn at the rear of their guardhouse.

"Hey, where's he gone?" asked Hector, seeing a definite empty space, with just an outline of crushed grass, where he had left the unconscious Keeper. "Surely no witches were this close?"

"He might have recovered faster than we expected," replied Steemer, "though that doesn't explain why he hasn't re-joined us."

"If he's nuts enough to charge on single-handed, we'll find out either from gloating witch celebrations and a fresh attack – meaning he's dead, or – if he's lucky enough to survive – he'll return, probably sometime tomorrow."

Chapter 8

MILITARY DISASTER

It was a real mystery. Two weeks had passed with neither a witch onslaught nor Keeper's reappearance. There was not even the third, unlikely option of a ransom demand turning up.

"Nature's more use to them alive than dead perhaps, but not him," thought Targah gloomily, who was really missing his older brother.

They had to assume the worst when a fair-sized attack was made on Malt Lake, a town situated halfway between Barleybag and Zog, the main witch territory. Many of the inhabitants were of dubious loyalty, legality, or morality, and this witch advance was doubtless designed to coerce by fear as many as possible to their evil way of thinking, at the same time burning and pillaging wherever they met any open defiance.

Tar Kang held a war council.

Hector spoke first: "We don't know why or how we've lost Keeper. If he's not among us within the next two months, I suggest we organize a lost-in-action memorial. Meanwhile, we must move on now and appoint a new leader. As Steemer runs the army, I vote we offer him the job."

"Are you willing to take it?" asked Digger, his younger brother.

"You must, starting right now!" It was Ducky who spoke: "I can now report an even bigger witch army gathering north of Malt Lake."

"What should we do?" asked Digger.

Steemer often wished his brother could put forward at least one creative idea, though he was rather stumped.

"We'd better attack," said Hector, "even if we're outnumbered. If we don't, they'll take the whole town and gather recruits."

"Yes… at least half of the Malt Lakers cannot be trusted," commented Digger. He spoke the same way as he dressed – quietly and immaculately. "And by attacking, we may be able to galvanize at least some of the Malt Lakers into helping us. Their sense of right and wrong is indeed hazy, but if we show them that we think we have a fair chance of victory, they may wish to share the glory."

"I don't like the odds," said Ducky bluntly. "I've seen how many there are."

"Suppose we mobilise just southeast of Malt Lake, to begin with," suggested Targah. "Then we could send out some scouts to gauge the mood of the Malt Lakers while Ducky and friends do more aerial surveillance."

"OK," said Ducky, "but remember: we can't see **everything** from overhead, especially where there are thickly clustered buildings or woodland."

Of the available options, Targah's plan seemed the safest.

Steemer concluded: "Let's get moving."

Jim and Ted briefed their units regarding the mobilization plans.

"It may get messy," said Jim.

"We'll need our wits and lots of courage," warned Ted.

Most of the big cats greeted the possibility of a big fight with loud enthusiasm. So did the bigger, but not very bright, bears. Before long, the pick of Barleybag's military volunteers was amassed within sight of Malt Lake.

Ducky whizzed down. "Bad news, I'm afraid. Speedy, the giant condor, spotted a number of witch hats at this end of Malt Lake. It seems they have infiltrated already."

"Well, thank Speedy for me," answered Steemer.

"I can't. He was shot down by a witch sniper's crossbow."

"I'm so sorry. And it seems that we'll have to attack at once."

A flank of the enemy forces was visible to the north of the town.

Steemer raised his rifle.

"Sound the slow advance, but do it very quietly," he instructed the bugler bear: "that way, we may catch some of them off guard."

He now led the way, pointing his rifle forward, and their whole formation moved ahead as quietly as possible. They managed to sneak quite close, in some cases crouching low, using the shadows of the houses at the left and the undergrowth at the right. Then, a few witches turned round and peered against the low sun. Seeing Steemer, they did a war dance.

Unperturbed, the Tar Kang leader shouted: "Charge!"

His bugler blew fortissimo, and their troops rushed headlong into battle.

"Geronimo!" yelled Steemer, knocking two opponents off their broomsticks with his raised rifle.

"Look out, Targah!" yelled big brother Hector, noticing a witch with a vicious dagger in the shadow of an overhanging tree branch. "Over your head!" he added.

In a single smooth movement, Targah calmly unholstered his jungle pistol and fired twice. With a horrendous screech, the witch fell into a mess of ferns and nettles.

The bear unit, led by Ted, Barney, Bluey, One-Eye, and Ozzie, closed in on the black witches, who were under the command of Witch Tiger.

"Don't rush ahead of the rest!" Barney warned Taresplit, a young recruit.

Some air cover came from Ducky's contingent, several armed like their leader, with shields and lances. Genies were battling against spooks.

Jim, Niger, Sata, and the other cats exchanged blows with Thuga and the other iron witches.

Suddenly, Hector spotted a sight that chilled his spine.

"That's Tiptoes!" he gasped. "He's walking death!"

As if to confirm Hector's fears, the pink-mauve semi-translucent witch touched one animal or human after another, causing instant fatality in most cases.

"What can we do?" asked Niger while adroitly dodging another witch's lunge.

Tar Kang forces were retreating in panic and not much order. Then, they noticed a small, smiling jellyfish advancing against the tide of fugitives.

"There's one creature at least that's not afraid to die – or just dead stupid," said the fascinated Targah.

"Hey!" uttered Niger: "See Tiptoes' face now!"

The look of fixed malevolence had changed – unbelievably – into abject terror.

Then, the deadly witch vanished.

"My scouts and spies gave me info' on this dreadful witch," said Steemer. "His poisonous touch, thankfully, only lasts in bursts, fifteen minutes max. And though he can swiftly switch from visible to invisible, he's only able to kill when we can see him. Also, I was told that there was one creature of which Tiptoes has a tremendous though irrational fear, but I just didn't believe it … until now."

"Let's not rejoice too soon," said Hector: "The disorder of our troops means that some of us stand a strong risk of being cut off from the rest."

"You're right," answered Steemer. "Niger, as the best dodger here, see if you can get to Monkey. If he's unhurt, I'm sure he can organize reinforcements."

Niger moved off, zigzagging past several would-be assailants.

"What other casualties does anyone know of?" asked Ted as he parried a wicked thrust from one of Witch Tiger's men.

"A number of our friends have been facing real peril," said Jim. "I could hear that Neddy was in distress; Squeaker had blood all over him; Croc and Fizzy looked anything but happy. That vile little ruffian Tadpole was astride some sort of airborne vacuum cleaner and dropping flasks of sulphuric acid... I think I'd better shut up." With that, he flattened two iron witches.

Then, with sickening realisation, Steemer witnessed the smile of triumph on Witch Crag's face.

"It's all been a carefully planned trap!" he muttered through clenched teeth.

Yes, a circle of witch archers now surrounded this small group of Tar Kang fighters that hadn't withdrawn in time. Red, one of the most loyal big bears, growled in rage and rushed at the enemy. He flattened one archer but then went down with two arrows in his throat.

"It is futile to resist," said Crag, coming forward. "Throw down your weapons, or you die in the next few seconds."

Jim glanced at Steemer, who nodded and dropped his rifle.

"They haven't killed us instantly; so let's hope the delay gives us an opportunity," he whispered.

"OK," said Hector, "but it could mean a slow, tortuous death instead of a quick one."

"We'll have to chance that. While there's life, there's hope."

"I'll try to remember that when they're pulling my teeth out."

Furball, a young lion, clearly shared the feeling and, catching the archers by surprise, made a sudden break through the cordon. It was to no avail. Jim shut his eyes and clenched his fists as he heard the dying growls.

"We all surrender," said Steemer quickly, though he was now speaking for only ten survivors.

"I've been wounded," said Ducky. "Can someone carry me?"

They were led to Spawn Grange, taken to a deep dungeon area, and secured in two adjoining cells.

Chapter 9

CAPTIVES AT SPAWN GRANGE

"Was it worth it?" asked Jim dolefully.

"It certainly doesn't seem so" said Hector carefully. "We lost some good men and courageous animals. If we can't get out of this dungeon, our heads may be off before you know it, and with Tar Kang's forces so depleted, not only will Malt Lake be taken – if it isn't already – but Barleybag too will be defenceless."

"Monkey may be able to help," said Targah.

"I wouldn't count on it. I saw Tiptoes touch his cape – or wand. There was a massive pink flash, knocking Monkey back about four meters, and he jerked, then just lay on the ground."

"So, we'd better think hard for any possible means of escape," Said Ted; "And we've probably got very little time."

"Yes," put in Barney: "I overheard one of the witches who locked us in talking to his comrade. It seems that Storm, chief of the red witches, is away with Spawn at a torture and black magic conference; so our fate is being postponed until they get back."

"And maybe they'll be itching to try out their newly learned skills with us as guinea pigs," whimpered Taresplit.

"All right," said Steemer, quickly asking himself what Keeper would have done in this situation. "First, we need to list the obstacles we have to overcome to reach safety. Then we must delegate tasks according to special abilities."

"Quite," agreed Hector. "Ted, you have one of the best brains, particularly when it comes to memory and recall, and Targah is handy with a pencil. So, help him make a diagram in the dustiest corner or wall of this dungeon, showing as much as you can remember of the route by which they brought us here."

"But I've no pencil!" muttered Targah. "Never mind: I'll use my finger as a naughty kid would on the back doors of a dirty van or the windows of their school bus."

"We'll need two witch uniforms," said Jim.

"What use is that?" growled Hector. "There are six of us in this cell."

"And four next door."

"How do you know who's next door? Can you see through the wall? Remember: the witch guards shoved us in here first. Where they put Sata, Ducky, and the others is anybody's guess."

"I'm not just guessing. I thumped on the wall in Morse code, and Sata replied. Scruffy and Boo are in there too."

"OK – we'll plan with them in mind."

"Just a minute," said Steemer. "I think I'm on your wavelength, Jim. Spell it out, please, for the benefit of the whole group – but quietly so that no witch guard can hear."

However, instead of doing as asked, Jim whispered in his ear. The others remained puzzled.

After a few minutes, Steemer explained: "Any one of us may get hauled outside for interrogation. If we each know only the minimum we need, then our plans will be safer."

Targah's map was now complete; so the others stared at it carefully, doing their best to commit it to memory. In case any guards should look through the cell bars and wonder what was up, Targah and Ted now stood between their friends and the door, chatting about nothing in particular.

"Do you know what happened to the magician who swallowed some furniture polish?" asked Targah.

"No. What?"

"He varnished!"

After a few minutes, Ted turned round, possibly to escape the jokes, and Steemer nodded to indicate that they were now ready.

Suddenly, Taresplit shouted: "I don't want to be tortured! I'm going to tell them where our treasure is!"

"Shut up, you little coward!" said Jim, "or I'll spiflicate you."

"Cowards live longer," put in Ted, "but not always. Taresplit, you could be the exception. You're a disgrace to the name of bear."

As it got noisier, the witch guard outside heard the bit about treasure and greedily beckoned his mate. "Quick, Sulphurous, let's get that turncoat before they kill him. He can make us rich!"

They unlocked the cell door, trying to move fast but carefully. In the far corner was a rugby maul of bodies, under which Taresplit was howling: "You can't stop me! I'm going to tell!"

"OK," said Witch Grog, clicking a gun and waving a curved dagger. "Get up and stand against the wall, all of you!"

Gradually, the jumble of bodies was disentangled and very clumsily, with many bumping into one another in apparent panic or with three trying to claim the same spot against the wall at the same time.

"Hurry up," screeched Grog, "or you're all dead!"

Sulphurous was now counting the prisoners: "Four, five… but?"

Then, both witches lost consciousness.

Hector emerged from the shadows behind these falling guards whose heads he had banged together.

"Got their keys?" asked Steemer.

"Nope. I think they left them in the lock."

Like a flash, Taresplit confirmed it. "Maybe I'll lock you all in for the pounding you gave me," he quipped.

"It had to look realistic," replied Jim: "the guards weren't complete morons."

"Then why are you smiling behind your paw?"

Meanwhile, Steemer and Targah dressed themselves in the witch outfits while Hector and Ted bound and gagged the two unfortunate guards and shoved them into the corner where the (now erased) dust map had been.

"Quick march!" ordered Targah in as witchy a voice as he could muster. "Open the next cell!"

The new 'Sulphurous' did so, winking at the four animals inside.

"What an ugly witch!" said Scruffy, "and he's got something wrong with his eye."

Steemer gave him a good cuffing. "Just move your butt, you cheeky little horror. You've got an important assignment coming up."

He now turned to the others. "OK: everyone is to behave as prisoners of Targah and myself. If we meet any ultra-suspicious witches, Sata will come from the shadows to silence them. At my signal, Ducky will fly in the almost opposite direction, firstly, to cause a diversion, and secondly, to get back to Barleybag for any reinforcements he can find.

"But Ducky's wounded and lame!"

"No, he's not. You were just pretending, weren't you, Ducky, so as to stay with us and improve our chances of escape. Am I right?"

"Oh well," confessed Ducky, "... at least my acting fooled the witches."

"Assuming we succeed in reaching the moat, you, Scruffy, will get your assignment, and you must act without hesitation."

"Yes, boss."

Boo now gave Taresplit a relatively gentle bop and, while he was off balance, relieved him of the key. Then he locked the two cells behind them.

"Good thinking," said Hector. "That will delay discovery for a while."

"I think his only motive was revenge on the guards," muttered Jim.

"Now keep talk to a minimum, except whispers," said Steemer, then in witch voice, "No talking amongst the prisoners!"

They moved down the pre-planned escape route, 'Grog' at the front, 'Sulphurous' stomping along at the back. They got through the torture room without difficulty, though Jim took the time to break apart three of the most fiendish machines, but in such a way that the damage would not be immediately visible. As they ascended the spiral staircase, an ugly witch with even uglier torture weapons in each hand was coming down.

"Where are you taking the prisoners?" he demanded.

Recognising the enemy, Targah replied, "Frog, these captives must be on the parade ground to be seen by Spawn and Storm on their return today."

"Today…?" Frog looked puzzled but continued his descent, that is, until Boo decided to bop him.

Slumped on the stairs, Frog yelled, "That crazy animal attacked me. Kill him!"

Jim promptly knocked the loud witch unconscious.

"All right," said Steemer: "this isn't the best place for our diversion, but we can use it. Ducky, as soon as Frog regains consciousness, shout,

"Wait for me!" loudly and head off to the right from the top of the stairs. Let's hope that Frog, along with any he summons to help him, follows you, either because he thinks I was lying about the parade ground or because Jim's blow knocked the memory out of his brain."

He now addressed the other 'prisoners': "Right, left, right, left!"

'Shouldn't it be left, right?' wondered Hector, then realised that witches did things differently.

They filed through the council room and down the main stairs to the parade ground.

Some witches came up to question their movements but then heard a loud shouting from Frog.

"Something's wrong!" snarled Crag and ran up the stairway, followed by most of his men.

One Witch, however, remained and stared at Targah.

"Who are you? You're not Grog."

"No – his replacement," said Targah quickly.

The disguised Steemer came forward. "Open the main gates at once," he commanded. "Spawn and Storm are due back any moment now and will be extremely angry if they are shut out because of your incompetence."

The Witch's face changed from suspicion to fright. "Help me then. All the rest seem to be chasing other prisoners who are somewhere at loose in the north tower."

"I understand," answered Steemer. "My colleague will watch these captives while you and I unbolt and shift the gates."

Then he turned to Jim and the rest, who wore suitable expressions of sullen gloom or abject terror, and hissed, "Flat on the ground, now!"

They obeyed with alacrity. Soon, the gates were wide open.

Chapter 10

FREEDOM!

"Phew! Storm will be pleased," said Steemer. "Put it there!" He offered his hand to the helpful Witch, then flattened him.

"Now, Scruffy, your task: get through the moat and swamp, but head for that tree on the bank. See it?" Steemer pointed over to the right. "Don't rush, but equally, don't stop for anything."

"Hooray!" cried the dog, and plunged into the loathsome waters.

"What about the snakes?" asked Ted as he watched Scruffy's head bobbing mid-stream.

"They'll probably enjoy his mucky company, but if any does bite him, I'm certain it will be the snake, not Scruffy, that suffers… And the swamp **is** safer than the risk of facing Crag's road patrol dogs."

"Yes, but only if we get across while the snakes are preoccupied," said Jim, lowering himself into the moat. "Yuk! What a stench!"

Despite a strong desire to throw up, they all made it to the safe opposite bank, a good fifty metres left of Scruffy and any reptiles.

Jim looked back. There was no sign of pursuit yet, but to his delight, he saw Ducky circling above the north tower, just out of range of the many missiles being thrown at him.

"I hope he can outfly them if they get on their broomsticks," said Ted, also looking around.

"I trust Ducky's judgment," said Steemer. "He's buying us time; so let's get to the cover of the woods as soon as possible. We'll avoid Malt Lake, as we don't know who can be trusted in that town at the moment."

"Several of them are hardened criminals," added Hector, "and that's not likely to change."

Jim interrupted: "Beckon Ducky now to join us. We're nearly at the woods."

Hector did so. The distant speck stopped its circling and flew off – in the wrong direction.

"What's he playing at?" asked Hector.

"Don't worry. Once out of their sight, he'll change direction and head here: you watch."

Sure enough, they shortly heard a whirring flap of wings, and Ducky landed.

"You're bleeding!" said Ted.

"Don't fret. It's just a scratch. I misjudged one archer."

"Nevertheless, we'd better get you back to town soon just in case the arrow was poisoned."

"I must tell you, though," Ducky was chuckling: "there was a witch there in green, which was odd, because I've only seen Crone wear that colour, and it wasn't her. Anyway, this must be about the clumsiest idiot in their ranks. I thought at first that he had seen you lot going the other way, but he followed and overtook Frog, yelling, "This way, troops!" Then, after falling over on the steps in his haste, getting in everyone's way, and frequently shouting 'DUCK!', which was not only unnecessarily obvious but slowed them down as they hit the floor in response, he dashed to the broomsticks stacked by the parapet with another rallying cry: "Let's cut off his escape!" And can you believe it? In his rush, he fell onto the broomsticks, causing most of them to fall over the battlement and down into the moat! Clearly angry with himself, he bashed one good remaining broomstick against the wall, shouting violent curses, so it broke in half, leaving only a rather dog-eared broom still useable. Undeterred, he snatched it up and rushed towards the armoury, shouting, "More spears and longbows, quick!"

They followed him until he turned, swearing vigorously and announcing, "It's locked! Which fool did that?" If I were in a soccer game, I'd love to see him on the other team. So you see, my diversion and escape proved relatively easy."

Chapter 11

TED AND A HUNCHBACK

Could the tip-off be trusted? Steemer felt the migraine responsibility of standing in for their lost leader. If the attack was imminent, they would need to intercept it fast. The other possibility was that this was a ploy to divert his troops away from their current defences.

He pressed the emerald button to contact Monkey – only in emergencies.

"What's up?" It was Monkey, thankfully prompt.

"Can you trace an attack from the northeast, skirting Targah's Forest?"

"Let me see…. Yes, camouflaged, but you are right: I should have spotted it. How did you know?

"Never mind. Get all your forces ready for defence stations because I'm heading over there with all instantly available volunteers and regulars to intercept those fiends."

The Tar Kang men and animals moved north and paused for breath at the corner of the forest.

"They'll be visible any second now," whispered Steemer. "You attack first, Ducky, so that they'll be looking skyward when our infantry hit them from the trees."

"OK."

The battle crash was deafening. Terrible screams, first of exultation, then fury, and at last agony came from the witch forces.

Steemer spotted an unfamiliar, hunchbacked, ugly-looking, greenish-faced enemy that was creeping behind Ted, who was too busy cleaving witches with his sword to glance back.

"Look out!" screamed the leader.

It was too late. The monstrous hunchback had tripped the small bear and pinned him to the ground.

Ted thought his end had come. Strange words were chanted into his ear, and then he was slumped motionless.

"Oh no!" cried Steemer, and Targah, who had also witnessed the fall of a good friend, ran forward to rescue Ted's body.

The renewed vengeful fury of Steemer's troops now really repulsed the enemy hordes. Suddenly, to his surprise, the green-faced character, whom he had been eyeing closely with a view to engaging in hand-to-hand combat, threw himself forward and whined, "I surrender."

"If the bear's really dead, your life is forfeit," said Steemer coldly.

It turned out that Ted was stunned but otherwise OK.

"Alright, Ted. You decide his… its fate."

To Steemer's surprise, Ted replied, "Don't hurt him. I think we could use this horrible creature as a fifth columnist."

Jim, his young lion friend, laughed gruffly. "We'll have to call you 'frenemies' then."

"What do you mean?"

"Well, it's not clear yet whether you will finish up as friends or enemies."

"Maybe both," said the hunchback quietly.

Chapter 12

A FIENDISH TRAP AND A STRANGE RESCUE

Bunny had an early breakfast of mashed carrot porridge, and lettuce washed down with Barli-Cola. Then he headed for the main exit of his burrow. To his surprise, it required a terrific shove just to open the door.

He screwed up his eyes at the bright dazzle. There was snow everywhere. The neat little house's name 'Bunny's Burrow' was half buried. Where small bushes had been last afternoon, there were now just bumps, as if they were asleep under the bed sheets.

Some footprints were visible where there used to be a path.

"I wonder if that was Ted. He often gets up early," thought the little rabbit.

It was mid-July, Australian winter, and much colder than usual. As Bunny shivered and closed the door again, thinking, "I must get my warmest scarf and bobble hat," a large envelope with sprinklings of snow on it fell by his foot. On it was just one word – URGENT.

No time to look for a letter opener – he just bit off a corner with his teeth, then ripped the envelope so fast that he slightly cut his paw on the edge of the paper. The note inside read,

Please hurry! From the cedar tree at the north corner of Targah's Forest, head directly east for two hundred metres. I desperately need someone to come to the rescue, or …

The rest of the note was missing because the paper was clearly torn even before Bunny had chewed it.

"Crumbs!" he thought. "I wonder if it could be Nature or Keeper? Why is there no name? Did anyone else get a note like this? Have I time to get some extra help before I dash to the scene? Surely, it can't be Ted in trouble if he's only just headed that way… Or, more likely, he got a similar note."

Bunny followed the directions swiftly. As he neared the last specified metre, he heard what sounded like a faint cry for help. The rabbit hurried forward, though careful to bleep his mobile's emergency red phone button, which would vibrate and light up the wristband that Monkey wore everywhere, meaning 'TROUBLE,' with Sat-Nav style information of Bunny's precise whereabouts and movements.

Then his heart jumped.

On a grassy hillock, his mouth gagged, Ted was hanging by his two paws from the boughs of a gnarled tree. He started shaking his head at Bunny as if to warn him not to get closer. Bunny looked around apprehensively … but it was too late. Several small black isosceles triangles were appearing… witch hats! … and a large group of witches arose from the long grass.

"Trapped!" thought Bunny, and after a short struggle, during which he managed to trip and disable two enemies, he was marched to a dip nearby, where, to his horror, he saw a number of his friends had already been caught.

"And this time, they've captured us without even having to fight!" he thought miserably. "I bet they won't delay killing us either."

Suddenly, a strange noise hit the air, and a weird shape flew close, silhouetted against the sun. The witches, utterly baffled, hesitated for a few seconds as jet streams of glimmering liquid shot towards them. The best word to describe them once hit by the jets would be – 'jellified,' for each was trapped in a large, gooey bubble.

One Witch, however, had quicker reflexes or better luck and seized the bound Scruffy (who had also walked into the witch trap), mounted a huge broomstick and zoomed into the sky with the now petrified dog.

The spaceship hovered; a panel opened, and a youth's face appeared.

"Hi! I'm Buster ..."

"Introductions can wait!" yelled Bunny. "Get after that broomstick! That Witch has grabbed Scruffy."

Buster didn't pause to ask who Scruffy might be. Just making sure that no one was directly behind the burning jet motors, he zoomed away at full rocket speed. His magnifying zoom monitor tracked the distant black dot representing what he fervently hoped was the disappearing Witch.

Either Scruffy's kidnapper smugly felt safe and had slowed down, or Sci-Fi was proving faster than medieval magic. Either way, Buster was gradually gaining.

"OK, Whiskey," he addressed his fellow traveller, a tartan-patterned Scottie dog: "how are we going to lift the prisoner?"

"Get close above them, preferably over water or soft ground. Then I'll jump with my lariat and parachute.

"Dodgy – but I can't this minute think of a better tactic. First, though, we need to catch up, and we may have superior speed, but if we're spotted, I think we could be outmanoeuvred. Broomsticks, as you know, are nimble, sneaky, and often unpredictable. Besides, it might be one with an extra velocity booster."

"Whoopee," muttered Whiskey.

Most broomsticks would not be equipped with rear-view mirrors: it was a big design problem, but either this witch kept a mirror in the hat-rim or, more likely, a sixth sense made her look round.

With a blood-curdling battle cry, she dived towards a cluster of trees.

"Bother!" Buster gritted his teeth and descended fast.

Suddenly, a thick burnt-tyre sort of smoke blew in front of his vision.

"Oh, oh … the octopus escape trick!

"I'll engage the power air blaster," he added. "I hope it won't dislodge our doggie friend, but we need to see ahead."

Whiskey didn't reply. This was because he had already spotted Scruffy's body being thrown off the broomstick as the witch needed less weight while trying to escape; so Whiskey hit the downward ejector and dropped like a bullet after the fellow dog. He left his parachute tug to the last possible second.

Meanwhile, as Buster feared, the witch zoomed down at increased speed and in a death-defying manoeuvre between the gaps in the trees. The skill and daring had to be admired. Still, in quick response, the experienced space pilot pressed his body-heat-detection control, which then indicated on the monitor the enemy's position as a moving red blob.

"Now try escaping," muttered Buster, "and you're running out of woodland cover."

As if in answer, the blob suddenly disappeared.

"What the devil…?"

Baffled, he brought the spaceship down just beyond the wood's edge, engaged auto-lock, and ran towards where he estimated the witch had vanished from his screen.

Then he saw the answer.

"Bother! I should have guessed. She knew the entrance of a tunnel and escaped on foot underground."

At a later date, he would learn that the adroit and elusive foe was Witch Crone. Their enmity would become very personal, and he would discover that besides broomstick aviation skills, she was a master spellmaker. Fortunately, his fellow astronaut Whiskey was also quite capable in that department.

And what had happened with the Whiskey/Scruffy situation?

The would-be rescuer was too late. Scruffy must have already landed somewhere, dead or badly injured. Whiskey rolled over commando style as he hit the ground, then quickly looked around.

A gloppy, squelching noise arose from the flat area on his left. What might be an extremely muddy paw was half visible.

"Just in case that's our friend…" thought Whiskey as he threw out his lariat, expertly pulling it tight over the suspected limb. He then gave a terrific jerk on the rope. A louder squelch followed.

"This is no good. If that's him, he's heavier than me," he reflected.

He saw a tough-looking tree trunk nearby; so he quickly tied his rope end firmly around it.

Then, with bravery at almost stupid level, he waded into the swamp, holding the rope when the mud started to get really deep. The doggie paw, if that's what it was, now vanished below the surface.

"Bother!" Whiskey grunted and, taking a massive breath, reached down fast, hoping to get some hold of the missing animal. He clutched onto something and pulled himself back vigorously along the rope.

To his immense relief, a muddy head emerged and loudly spluttered. Whiskey tugged again. Now, his hind paws touched hard clay. This gave him so much better leverage, and they were both soon safe on the frosted but solid terra firma.

"Pwugh!" panted Whiskey: "this mud stinks!"

He glanced at the other dog.

Scruffy appeared to be mesmerized and stuttered: "Goo… goo… goo…."

"What's the matter? You OK?" asked his concerned rescuer.

A daft smile was slowly spreading on the other's face. Then Scruffy spoke.

"Lovely, LOVELY mud!"

"What the…? Are you nuts? That mud nearly killed you."

Yes, it had cushioned the poor mutt's landing, but - if Whiskey hadn't lent a hand - it would have doubtless suffocated him.

"He's suffered trauma," thought Whiskey. "He can't think straight." So he didn't argue. Nevertheless, once they got back to civilization (McQuack's Diner, just outside Barleybag), Scruffy didn't share the urgent necessity of getting a thoroughly good wash.

Hector and Steemer were knocking back decaffs over a friendly game of Field Chess. Hector had just captured a knight and promoted his rook; so he was looking quite smug.

"I feel so inadequate without Keeper and trying to fill his shoes," admitted Steemer with a sigh of frustration. "Look, we've suffered significant setbacks and outright defeats by the witches lately. Also, how can anyone match what Keeper's done for Barleybag just in the last few months? He introduced large road signs for the big roundabouts, tax reductions for safer drivers, luminous stripes on all vehicles and pedestrian nightwear, obligatory big, clear house numbers, licensing for kitchen knives, hard labour community projects for delinquents, written text on all TV and computer programs, CCTV in all classrooms and lecture halls… Need I continue?"

"OK," replied Hector. "I get the point. I'm personally trying to adjust to having lost a great brother. But we have to manage the situation as it is. You have my full confidence and cooperation; so just carry on leading us as best you can."

Steemer brightened at this encouragement. "Hey, I have an idea. Why don't we give the witches a taste of their own medicine? I mean, this time, we'll lure them into a trap. If only we could pin down Spawn, we might find out what's happened to Nature."

Chapter 13

A BOLD PLAN

"We've had a few more ransom notes for Nature just lately," Steemer continued. "Unless they're bluffing, at least it means that she's still alive, but I'm guessing, now that Keeper is missing, presumed dead, she's no longer in herself any practical use to them. Short of any herbal secrets they may have forced out of her – most of which would be to heal, not harm – her only value to them is as bargaining currency."

"What was their last ransom demand?" Hector looked extremely tense.

Steemer looked at him steadily. "They want both of us in her place."

"From a military point of view, that's unthinkable."

"Yes, but they may be playing mind games. I figure that Spawn's consulted Witch Bat: she's their expert in psychological warfare."

"So what do you propose?"

"This could be our only chance to nail Spawn and, more importantly, rescue Nature."

Hector then whispered, "Hey, I think I just heard someone by the window. Whoever it was may have overheard our plans."

"Stop worrying, or you'll get me worried too. We're in Barleybag, not Malt Lake."

Nonetheless, Steemer bounded across and looked outside. "I think it was that 'frenemy,' the green hunchback. I still don't trust him. Anyway, this is the reply I've drafted to the ransom demand."

Senior Command

Tar Kang Military

1100 hrs: urgent

To Witch Spawn

Spawn Grange

Zog

We're interested in your ransom offer. Bring a small delegation to a neutral, open country. We thought you would probably want to do business somewhere like Malt Lake Park, seeing that most of the locals do not like us but seem to want to be your allies.

Unless we hear otherwise, Hector and I will be there, with a small company, at 1800 hours.

But bring Nature. That way, we shall know that she is alive, unhurt, and ready for what you propose.

Field General S. J. Hawkins

Page 2: P.S. Show Nature page 1 if you want, but not this postscript.

Tell her that she's being ransomed, but don't say 'swapped' because we know she wouldn't agree to that.

"Yes, I think they'll play ball," said Hector after a minute's thought. "But what happens at the rendezvous?

"I have a good trick up my sleeve," answered Steemer. "I just pray it will work. Come to my room in the officers' mess, where there's top security, and I'll put you fully in the picture."

Chapter 14

NATURE'S DEATH SENTENCE

The small Tar Kang group approached the entrance of Malt Lake Park. The witches were there already. A vindictive gloat flickered on Spawn's face. However, Nature was there, and Hector could tell that she looked tired but otherwise OK.

All around the park were Malt Lake people, some appearing utterly unconcerned, others crowding near the two converging enemy groups.

"You Barleybaggers never learn!" said Spawn contemptuously. "Instead of a swap, I think we'll just kill the whole pack of you. I see you brought that Jellyfish, but Tiptoes isn't here. Nevertheless, he'll be glad to know that we've dispatched his enemy."

"Brave and treacherous words," answered Steemer, seeing that you only count eight of us here, and you appear to outnumber us by about ten to one."

"To quote a famous Red Indian, 'today is a good day for fighting,'" said the witch leader.

"Yes, as long as it's extremely one-sided," said Hector. "But if that's what you want… "

All the Malt Lakers now revealed an assortment of deadly weapons.

"You see," explained Hector: "They're with **us**. These men may look like Malt Lake crooks, but in fact, they've come all the way from Barleybag."

Steemer now spoke. "All right, Spawn: you may as well give up. Hand over Nature now, and without fuss, and we'll allow you ten minutes to get lost."

The witches looked anxiously at their leader.

"You'll never get me," hissed Spawn coldly, then quickly pointed at Nature, malevolently ordering: "Kill her!"

Hector and Steemer froze with horror as the gleeful witches closed in on the helpless girl, though remaining wary of her powerful herbal 'magic.'

"Allow me!"

The hunchback spoke, stepping forward from behind Hector.

"Spawn, I've played a double agent long enough. Now, see my real loyalty. I'll rid you of this nuisance woman – permanently."

He drew an evil-looking curved and serrated knife.

Jim clenched his paws. Bunny raised a spear. Even Boo moved forward.

"He's mine!"

Ted advanced, sword at the ready.

"Hold it," said Hector to Targah, who had fitted an arrow to his bow. "Our bear feels guilty about recruiting that vile rogue; so let him sort it. Anyway, we might hit Ted by mistake."

He immediately regretted his advice as, with horror, they saw the curved blade flash down. Ted gave a short gasp, then moaned and slowly crumpled to the ground.

Now, the fiend had grasped Nature's wrist and, muttering in her ear with a sadistic expression, moved right behind her.

"You won't forget this:" The hunchback addressed Spawn with a twisted grin. "Fancy a closer look? Hurry up. My fingers are itching." He moved the knife in front of Nature's throat.

"Stop!" shouted Steemer. Have me instead! I'm more use dead to you than she is!" Simultaneously he nodded to Hector and made a clear thumbs-down signal.

Hector understood and looked at his girlfriend, May. She, as Nature's sister, would not take any stupid risks, but of all those he'd met, she happened to be the best shot with a rifle. Carefully lining up the telescopic sight, she aimed at the hunchback's knife arm, planning to smash the elbow and force release of the knife. Praying that Nature would not suddenly be moved, she softly squeezed the trigger... and again.

To her dismay and disbelief, the shots resulted in no change of situation.

"I can't have missed, surely?" she wondered.

She turned away, her mind refusing to witness Nature's execution.

Spawn stood by the traitor with cruel anticipation: "Well, get on with it then!"

The hunchback pulled back his arm, then suddenly sidestepped and was now at Spawn's throat.

"Freeze, all you witches or Spawn gets it – as messily as possible! And don't try anything stupid."

He turned to Nature: "Get over to our men, fast, while they're still puzzled."

In dazed bewilderment, Nature did so.

Now the hunchback relaxed his grip and addressed Spawn once more. "As our lady has remained alive and unharmed up till now, I'm letting you and your sorry band slither back to your buddies in Zog, but first, throw down all your weapons. At Witch Fort, they'll love to hear how you managed to lose your prize hostage and get outwitted by a small Tar Kang group and a deformed green outcast. Oh, and make sure you read this before you get to bed." He passed a folded note to his enemy.

A look of pure hate came over the witch leader's face. Without a word, he turned, dropped his sword and rifle, nodded to his men to do the same, then led them back out of the park and away, escorted a safe distance to the open bushland by the Barleybag commando unit which had successfully posed as Malt Lakers, and who now added to the witches' humiliation by lustily singing the Tar Kang anthem.

"You had us very worried," said Steemer to the hunchback. "especially as you clearly spiked our rifles – May's, anyway. But I'm sure glad you came through for us."

"A witch's capacity for hate can often overcome his better judgment," replied the hunchback. "Spawn's command to kill Nature was a classic example. Put today's events down to experience. Your fake Malt Lakers were a great idea. Don't blame yourself that the plan nearly went pear-shaped. You have been a great leader."

"What do you mean – 'have been'?" demanded Hector, who was finding the hunchback's remarks increasingly irritating. "He still is our leader."

"Not anymore," said the resurrected Ted. "You see, I've known well before this ugly creature attacked me: he's a very much disguised KEEPER... and we faked my dramatic death."

There was a stunned silence.

Then Keeper, for it was indeed he, straightened up and said, "Let's get back to Barleybag. I need to wash off this awful colour. Tonight, we'll have an amazing party!"

Chapter 15

WALKING THE DOGS

"Come on. We're taking the dogs for a walk."

"Fine!" it was a new experience for Keeper: "Now, you've told me all about them. Let me see: that's Bella, the plumper, more lightly coloured, naughty one? And Sasha's pretty much as I imagined."

Defensive barks met his words until he patiently endured boisterous doggy inspection.

"They stay on the leash," said Nature, "until we get away from the busy town roads."

Soon they reached open country, the edge of the Australian bush. A fresh, gentle breeze was starting up, and white explosions of cumulus cloud made slow ballet above them.

Nature's hair danced in the light. The dogs, now freed, raced off like Formula One greyhounds. Keeper watched in fascination as Sasha stopped under a fair-sized eucalyptus to yelp at a sleepy koala, though with no obvious effect. The call of a laughing jackass mocked her from the distance.

Bella had vanished into some far bushes.

It was peaceful sitting on a dry grassy mound, enjoying the changing landscape and chatting about so many things.

The novelty for Sasha of barking at the koala, which was as responsive as a woolly winter hat, had soon worn off, so Keeper threw her a short stick, calling "Fetch!", sometimes aiming it one way then hurling it in an entirely different direction to test the dog's ability to think fast and alter course.

"I wonder what happens when locals with dogs throw boomerangs around?" he mused aloud.

"First, the stick would land at your feet; then, the dog would probably collide with you," suggested Nature cheerfully.

"Thank heaven for beagles. If anyone had a St Bernard and a boomerang, he'd no doubt get steam-rollered at fifty miles per hour."

"I'd better call Bella," said Nature. "That blessèd dog can be very naughty sometimes and ignore my call."

"Now, would I ever do that?" put in Keeper.

She cried out louder than her companion had yet heard her: **"Bella! Here, you naughty dog... BELLA!"**

The response was entirely unexpected:

"Over here, quick! Help me!"

"Crumbs!" muttered Keeper: "I didn't know Bella could talk!"

"That's not Bella, silly, but it sounds as if someone's in real trouble," answered Nature.

They ran towards the voice, Sasha leading the way. There was a scurry in the undergrowth near a jacaranda tree.

A very weathered character, looking like the hobo in 'Waltzing Matilda' or one of McCubbin's outback tramps, emerged and dropped on his knees before the surprised Nature.

"Don't let them get me, please!"

"Don't let who?"

"The Rangers are after me because I've taken some diamonds."

"Well," said Keeper, "that's hardly surprising. Anything you steal needs to be given back."

"But you don't understand …. There's a multi-dollar gems syndicate forcing small prospectors into starvation by monopolizing sales, and we are held over a barrel to surrender our rough uncut gems, dug out with blood, sweat, and tears for rock-bottom prices."

He paused and gasped for breath.

"And who are you?" asked Nature, her eyes widening in wonderment.

"Ah, sorry – the name's Bruce Daniels. Very pleased to meetchah."

"Look," interrupted Keeper agitatedly: "we'd better get you somewhere safe till we can sort out your problems."

Chapter 16

ON THE RUN

"Follow me," said Nature, almost disappearing over a sandy mound into the bed of a small brook.

"Ssssh!" she addressed the two dogs – Bella had finally appeared and was fussing around their new acquaintance.

"I shared a dry biscuit and some homemade jumbuck paté I had left," said the prospector; "so I guess she's taken a shine to me."

"That dog's always scrounging – but she's really too plump, you'll find."

They followed Nature's lead, who had now hoisted her skirt and was wading vigorously downstream.

"If the Rangers have dogs too, they'll maybe lose our scent if we stay in the water for a while," she explained. "And this should bring us into Targah's Forest soon, where we can hide better or get your brother's help."

The last remark was made to Keeper, who knew that Targah had made his home there, part in, part under, a giant tree near the jungle-like heart of the very large woodland area.

Their eyes had to adjust quickly to the relative darkness provided by the several trees.

"Hey, what's that?" asked Keeper.

A quite large dark shape was now bearing down on them. As it got closer, two fierce eyes were visible. Bella yelped and dived behind Nature's soggy dress. Sasha stood transfixed.

Then Keeper laughed. "It's Sata. He's Jim's panther friend, and Targah lets him work as a guardian forester."

"Oh, that's a relief," said Nature, though an involuntary shudder still ran down her spine as the hotly breathing nightmare-like creature suddenly stopped barely a metre before them.

A whimper came from the half-hidden Bella.

"I thought DOGS were supposed to chase CATS," teased Bruce, who, even in crisis, had a wry sense of humour.

Nature's eyes flashed: "Leave the poor dog alone!"

"There could be armed Rangers catching up with us soon." Keeper addressed the panther. "Could you distract them for a while?"

Sata nodded without any hesitation: in fact, from his twisted grinning teeth it seemed that he relished the idea of a bloodthirsty scrap.

Leaving the brave panther between them and their fast-approaching pursuers, Keeper led the way deeper into the forest. As it grew darker, Sasha and Bella stopped dashing about and stayed very close to Nature's legs, almost tripping her over. She glanced back upon hearing a high hissing growl from Sata.

"What was that for? Any idea?" she asked Keeper. "Surely he's not telling them which way to come!"

"I guess it's rather a signal to **our** friends: that panther is ultra-loyal. Anyway, the Rangers might pacify but would hardly shoot a large cat."

Nature was still quite concerned, but they continued, hastily but also more carefully, away from the noise that was rumbling behind them.

Then, an eerie cacophonous high-pitched cackling noise echoed through the trees.

"That doesn't sound like Rangers," said Keeper with a worried frown.

As it happened, there was a forest fire watchtower ahead on the left.

"Quick! I'm going to check it out."

The "quick" must have been addressed to himself as Keeper gate-vaulted the perimeter fence and raced up the steep ladder steps until at treetop level.

There was no doubt. Dark shapes in the air – these were not Rangers. Somehow, someone had informed the witch command of their whereabouts. He shinned back to the ground.

"Sata will be dead meat. I'll go back. You carry on."

"Two of you against all of them - that's still suicide." Nature was dogmatic.

"If we move fast, the cat can be saved." It wasn't Keeper speaking but a newly arrived friend, Jim the Lion. "Sata's call came through, and the cavalry is here."

Chapter 17

IN TARGAH'S FOREST

Jim and a troop of big cats, including some whose names they later learned - Annis, Niger, Stripes, and Dad Lion – plunged past towards the lone fighting panther. Following them was a weird array of armed robots.

The witch horde had by now reached the solitary big cat.

"Stand aside or die!" cried Witch Storm, one of the leaders.

For a moment, Sata did not reply. Then he slowly purred, "What do you want? This is not your forest."

"We've tracked Keeper Jackson – and we'll get him."

"Dead or alive," piped up another witch: "… dead, preferably."

"I warn you. It won't be just me you'll have to deal with," growled Sata. "I advise you to leave while you still can."

"Brave words!" Storm sneered: "I can only see one sorry cat."

Sata bared his teeth and gave a loud, menacing snarl.

"Kill!" Storm curtly commanded.

As two super-enthusiastic broomstick riding witches zoomed straight towards his head, Sata backed almost imperceptibly about five yards. Too late, the witches realised their mistake as the panther ducked beneath some now very close branches, and both attackers squashed themselves on the trees.

Howls of fury arose as the rest closed in.

The timing could hardly have been better. It was like a movie: a fearsome group of feline and mechanical adversaries appeared from the shadows and hurtled into the astounded witch troops.

Dad Lion swung his walking stick to knock an airborne witch off her broomstick, then, using his full weight, prodded a ground fighter on the foot, causing an excruciating yell.

Niger would stand motionless until an opponent nearly reached him and then somehow sidestep so fast that the lunging enemy lost balance and fell forward or collided with another witch.

Jim was enjoying himself, using his sizeable furry but tough paws to punch any foe within arm's length.

Annis was quite a softie, but his imposing stature and fierce look made many witches fall back in fright and so hurriedly that they knocked over those behind them, making what looked like a very messy rugby maul or collapsed scrum.

One large robot, which they later learned was called Howling Horror, moved between four or five witches, then set off explosions as if each arm was tossing small grenades or dynamite sticks. Various bits of broomsticks, witch hats, and shattered weapons rained into the air wherever it (noisily) moved.

Storm decided it would be wisest to sound the retreat. He signalled with a triple blast on a modified goat horn. The witches instantly rushed away, those with broomsticks soon looking like swarms of demented locusts against the sky.

Sata took a deep breath, dug his claws into a witch that lay prostrated beneath him, then hugged and shook paws with the friends who had come to the rescue.

"They might have beaten us through strength of numbers," reflected Niger.

"Ah, yes," replied Jim, "but notice a key difference: they fight for sport and cruel delight; we fight by nature out of necessity, for food and survival."

"True," agreed Sata, "yet we can still have fun at the same time!"

The three cats now, with Jim leading, started to sing the new national anthem:

"All gentle creatures,

Join us in song:

This is our homeland,

Where we belong.

"Witches nor wizards

Can us dismay:

Tar Kang shall conquer;

Here we will stay.

"Ring out the anthem;

Proudly we fight,

Raising our flag for

Freedom and right."

"Why are we called Tar Kang?" asked Sata in his deep bass voice.

"I believe it's because soon after getting here TARgah caught and tamed a large KANgaroo," explained Niger.

Meanwhile, Keeper, Nature, Bruce, and the two dogs had been met by Targah.

"Hi, bro," he addressed Keeper. "Come to the tree-house and have a good rest. You look as though you need it."

"Dead right," said Nature. "I'm shattered."

"This is our new friend, Bruce," explained Keeper. "He's in trouble with the law… but it's some greedy and dodgy mining cartel that's really to blame. He was being chased by Rangers, but either the witches discovered my whereabouts and scared them off or …"

"… or the cartel made a deal with the witches," put in Bruce, "thinking they would kill us all, no questions asked. Rangers have scruples and a code of honour: witches don't.

They came to a massive old tree in the heart of the forest. Targah pressed his fingerprint on his mobile's screen, causing a camouflaged door to open in the heavily barked trunk. A spiral staircase was revealed. He tapped again, and a light came on inside the door.

"Quick!" he urged. "Go up to my lounge."

They all did as requested, Nature and Keeper each carrying an exhausted dog. They ascended into a timber-boarded, beautiful room with four neat, curtained windows looking out between thick branches across the forest. In the corner was another stairway, straight this time, which led up to further accommodation.

"My! You've certainly been working hard," Keeper complimented his brother. "But I'm wondering: what if an enemy found your home?"

"It could be awkward," admitted Targah. "Outside, I have impregnated the tree bark with gallons of fire-proofing chemicals. If all else failed, there's an escape route through the treetops to a safe-house second home."

They were treated to a lovely meal: some of it was forest produce – woodland mushrooms, chestnut paste, bramble dessert, but Targah had made himself a couple of fenced areas about 500 metres away, where he grazed a few goats and grew various fruit trees and vegetables.

"Duck Mart brings in other goods as needed, or I take the Land Cruiser into Barleybag for provisions," explained Targah cheerfully.

A generator camouflaged in a dense thicket supplied electricity. Two forest waterfalls gave hydro-electric power, and there were three wind turbines, they learned, all guarded by grills so that there would be no risk to passing birds.

"I can lower the grills by remote control should any foolhardy witches fly low over the trees. If they don't dodge the turbines, they know it can be quite messy." Their host grinned.

Bruce now stood up and reached into his old coat pocket, producing a rough leather pouch.

"I want to thank everybody," he said with slow emphasis, "and I insist on letting this young man take as a mark of my gratitude this small item, as long as he promises to pass it on to that lovely lady who's with him." So speaking, he passed the pouch to Keeper. "Don't open it yet. Wait till the next time you both go out for a stroll."

"Sounds exciting," said Nature, eyes shining happily. "Thank you anyway."

"Wait, we're not out of the woods yet," said Keeper, "… if you'll excuse the expression!" He grimaced at Targah. "It's **lovely** being here. But we need to discover where this diamond cartel HQ may be and get them off your back, Bruce, permanently."

Chapter 18

SEEKING JUSTICE

It was a fair trip to Sydney by train. Sometimes, Keeper and Nature just held hands; sometimes, he laid his head on her lap or she on his. A few roughnecks who entered the carriage at Melbourne smirked, but it didn't matter.

After a long but picturesque journey, the train pulled in at Sydney Central. Nature examined the city map on her iPad.

"How about we meet at Hurricane Grill near Bondi Beach?" (She indicated it with her finger.) "We can text or phone to sort out the time."

"Fine! Let's hope we both survive the next few hours. After all, we're taking on the big guns."

"Yes. In fact, you'd better wait for my all-clear before you do your bit."

"Just give me a quick hug first… in case it all goes wrong."

After a five-minute clinch, Nature walked purposefully toward the National Office of Fair Trade, an imposing neo-Gothic edifice in the heart of the city.

"This must be one of the oldest buildings in the country," she thought, looking up to where over the door stood a bronze statue of Justice, a blindfolded lady holding scales and a sword.

"I think someone's near your door and about to cause trouble," Nature told the receptionist. "It may be nothing, but I think you'd better take a look."

The smartly dressed youth jumped from his desk and quickly came to her side. He hesitated a moment. "I can't see anything."

"No, you're looking the wrong way. It was just round to the left, on the pavement right near one of your windows. Can't you hear something? Perhaps …."

He dashed outside.

As soon as he moved out of her line of vision, Nature quickly passed the inside doors and ran across to the big stairway, where she snuck behind a large curtain so that she was now invisible from the entrance but could observe the ground floor and first-floor main office areas. Reaching in her handbag for her small but powerful binoculars, she read some of the door plaques.

While she was trying to decipher the names and job descriptions, suddenly, three men appeared heading for the exit, the first red-faced and overweight, the second rather sallow and pasty, the third wizened and furtive.

Click!

"That might prove useful," she said to herself as she checked her new mobile phone photo.

Keeper entered 'Van Groot Quality Gems', an impressive jewellery emporium with a triple-length window display – bullet-proof glass probably.

"Could I have a quick word with the manager, please?" he asked. "It's quite important."

He was shown into a small but neat office, where a trim, earnest-looking gentleman with a pencil-sized moustache and hair brushed back almost symmetrically sprang up from a velvet-armed teak chair. "I'm very busy. What's this about?"

"The authorities are about to crack down on unethical wholesalers." Keeper was garnishing the facts in anticipation of Nature's mission proving successful. "You can probably escape trouble if you cease dealing with those diamond merchants that are facing investigation… at least till the smoke clears."

"But how will I know which dealers to avoid?" half stuttered the clearly rattled manager.

"Recognise any of these?"

Keeper held his mobile forward with the picture that Nature had emailed to him.

"Why yes. That's Dimitri Britten." He indicated the pasty-faced man. "He represents the Blue Diamond syndicate."

"Got their address?"

"Uh… no…."

The name did not appear when Keeper googled it.

"Apart from arriving on your premises, how else have they contacted you?"

"They phoned my mobile two or three times."

"Oh, good!" answered Keeper, with some relief and a glimmer of hope. "Can I borrow that phone?"

He started hacking.

After about five minutes, he'd discovered a location, a warehouse on the North Side.

"Thanks!" He grinned, handing back the mobile: "You should be safe from the law now."

With that, Keeper left the bemused businessman and stepped outside, where, conveniently, there was a choice of taxis.

At Keeper's urgent hail, an Asian gentleman lowered his window.

"Where to, sport?"

Keeper gave the street reference.

"Dodgy area, but… what the heck? Climb aboard."

As Keeper was dropped off, the cabbie commented, "Sooner you than me, mate."

Chapter 19

NATURE'S PROPOSALS

"I'm glad I didn't bring the two dogs with me," thought Nature as she entered the big ground floor executive office vacated by the three shady characters and felt rather like the small lad in the painting 'When Did You Last See Your Father?'.

She took a deep breath and fastened her eyes on the least fierce-looking of the five officials lining the other side of a heavy, polished oak table.

"Who might you be, young lady?" asked the central figure.

"You won't know me, but that doesn't matter. I represent the hard-working, independent miners who slog their guts out in this country to extract precious stones. They are being systematically exploited by giant cartels, which have been creating monopolies on various minerals. Examine what's happening with diamonds, for instance. Wouldn't you like better value and a clear conscience if you were buying a lady a beautiful diamond ring? Surely you'd be upset if you found it might have cost the blood of a poor small miner!"

"So; what do you propose?"

"I'm asking that a fair trade certificate be issued with each jewellery item sold; also that cartels be investigated and monitored, subject to unannounced inspections of premises and accounts – both company and personal – as deemed necessary; that minimum rates should be in force for what wholesalers pay the miners for their raw gems according to their purity scale and gram mass; that sufficiently harsh fines or imprisonment may be an effective deterrent; that known exploiters be named and shamed in the press and industry. One bad company, I am led to believe, currently trades under the name of 'Blue Diamond.'" (Nature paused for breath.)

"But that's… "

"Let me guess. The men who just left represent that syndicate."

"Er, that is indeed the case. However, they complained that a miner by the name of Daniels, aided by a certain Mr. Jackson and Miss Langton, had stolen diamonds that were rightly theirs."

"Poppycock! And in case you haven't guessed, I am Miss Langton, and you can check my person, premises, and bank accounts. I don't have handfuls of diamonds. I wish I did! Over the last few weeks, I've been working in a restaurant behind the bar, and before that, I did some ancillary nursing – just to balance my finances and keep a roof over my head. Would I have bothered if I had a secret fortune stashed away? Spending money for my annual holiday, if I get one, is tightly budgeted.

"Do you see the picture?

"And don't let anyone dare question the integrity of Mr. Jackson. He is respected by everyone in our community and is now an acknowledged, capable, and scrupulously fair leader.

"Check me. Check them. I pray that the truth will come out. Australia cares for the little guy. It champions him against the big bullies and against those shifty, weasel-faced conmen who bribe with backhanders to get their way and trample over others, securing for themselves positions where they can fleece hundreds of ordinary Joes."

The three men and two women facing Nature now conferred hurriedly and passed scribbled notes. She waited in dignified silence, hoping that her impassioned words had made some useful impression.

Suddenly the chairman jumped to his feet: "You are asking us to trust the word of one individual rather than an established business organisation?!"

Then, equally quickly, his eyes glazed over, and he slumped back in his seat. The others had the same dazed, rather stupid, and dreamy expressions, seeming to look past Nature towards the door.

She turned around. There stood Monkey, resplendent in his deep blue coat and small coned hat. His wand was making a slow vertical circle, and his eyes had a bright green light that made her feel rather dizzy.

Something seemed to click in the chairman's brain. Now, he spoke in a calm, collected tone. "We will indeed investigate these matters very carefully. One thing you can be assured of anyway – any business cartel that is as powerful as you suggest could be a danger not only to individual workers but to the government itself. Therefore, we will bring in some extremely strict controls and sanctions. We will also ensure in the next few days that the 'Blue Diamond' syndicate is thoroughly checked out, not only in regard to business procedures and ethics but also for any traces of illegal and criminal activities."

"I'm convinced," Nature replied quietly but clearly, "that they tried to get Mr. Daniels killed, along with Mr. Jackson and myself, and that they made a deal with a gang of psychopaths who dislike us intensely, resenting our presence ever since we arrived in this country. If I get any evidence to support my allegations, I'll send it to you. Thank you for listening. Goodbye for now."

She glanced at Monkey with a puzzled smile; then they both walked briskly out of the door, and she sent a fast text to Keeper's mobile: 'All clear. B careful. C U soon XXX.'

"That official was about to take me apart," she addressed Monkey. "What did you do – hypnotise him?"

"You guessed ... but in a rather special way."

Chapter 20

WELL MEANT BUT STUPID

Keeper found an inconspicuous spot in a corner out of the light, which was not too difficult, as the streets here were quite narrow. He guessed from the timing of Nature's latest text that the three stooges in the photo she'd sent earlier would be arriving back at their HQ shortly and that it would probably be in one of the buildings across the road from where he stood.

Sure enough, he soon spotted a dark-windowed black sedan cruising to a halt about twenty metres away. Two men emerged: one, he deduced, was the chauffeur; the other, judging by his immaculate tailored suit and imperious manner, was possibly the Mr. Big of the outfit. His hunch proved even more justified when another, less flashy, vehicle drove up, disgorging three characters, quickly recognizable as matching the pic on the mobile.

Speedily donning some mafia-style sunglasses, he walked up behind them to the same open door that the presumed boss had just entered. As he essayed to follow, a burly henchman barred his way.

"I've got a large diamond to show the boss," said Keeper, "and he gets five minutes of my time, or I take it elsewhere; so; if you don't want to face his wrath, you'd better step aside fast."

The doorman's expression – solid bone between the ears – started to show some signs of confused agitation.

"OK," he said eventually, "… but you'll come out in a box if you're spinning me a lie."

Keeper's blood chilled, but he kept moving, trying to appear nonchalant. He was a little concerned about the twitch he had discerned in the big bruiser's eye… Had that been a wink at the last, rat-faced stooge? Or was he just being paranoid?

"I've set out to do something," he told himself obstinately; "so I'll see it through…," adding, "if at all possible."

One nagging doubt remained: would it be worth the trouble? He sincerely hoped so.

A few shabby, door-separated, and dimly gas-lit corridors led to a bigger, steel-reinforced door. Keeper rapidly followed the stooges through before it shut with a convincing thud.

In a plush armchair at the far side of an elegantly decorated room was the smartly dressed boss, chrysanthemum in lapel, oily hair groomed back, pock-marked jaw half disguised with powder, and a thin scar over his right eye. A bottle of red wine stood on a nearby mahogany table, along with four or five Venetian glasses, accompanied by a green malachite ashtray and a matching box of Cuban cigars.

"I believe this might interest you," said Keeper, advancing with a sizeable crystal sparkling in the open palm of his right hand.

An involuntary look of cunning greed came over the man's features, which he then endeavoured abruptly to hide.

'This is the big moment,' thought Keeper, and as the man reached forward, saying, "May I take a closer look?" our well-meaning hero quickly drove his left fist with full force into the criminal's surprised face.

As Keeper anticipated, after a few seconds of stupefied shock, the cronies moved towards him, hands in gun pockets, breathing menace.

"You're dead, punk!" promised weasel-face.

Keeper quickly spun about, hurling the mace and pepper bomb from his sleeve.

A cacophonous bedlam of sneezes erupted, along with much clutching at burning eyes.

Unfortunately, Keeper forgot the maxim 'Quit while you're ahead' and started ferreting about for any documentary evidence he could take away. Thus, he was too engrossed to notice that the big bouncer from the entrance area had missed most of the 'bomb' effect and was bearing down behind him with a malignant grin. Keeper turned as he heard a soft rustle in the carpet, but it was too late.

Chapter 21

A RESCUE

The next second, he was pushed against the wall, the intricate hard frame of a large painting (of the boss) digging into his spine, and the malevolent bully starting to slowly crush the life out of him.

Suddenly, there was a loud howl of agony, apparently from just outside the room. Even the sadistic thug guessed that Keeper was no ventriloquist, and so, scorning his victim, he turned round, struck by curiosity. The next moment, with a shattering noise, a hole appeared in one of the big door's solid oak lower panels.

Jim's paw, then a face appeared: the door juddered, then, its hinges completely broken, fell forward, smashing the wineglasses, breaking the small table, and even cracking the toughly made cigar box.

The big man stood in fixed astonishment as if paralysed - but not for long….

Keeper had observed that the carpet was still free of the fallen door. Flashing through his mind came the memory of a school delinquent who got expelled for pulling the carpet from under the feet of the aged headmaster, who was about to cane him. Inspired by this idea, Keeper yanked the carpet with all his might, causing his would-be tormentor to lose balance and crash down at the feet of Buster, who had now joined his young lion friend in the room.

It was just as well: the four other criminals had now recovered from the pepper and mace. Weasel Face pulled a gun on Jim … big mistake. The resourceful cub had grabbed the largest piece of a broken cigar case and hurled it so accurately at the man's forehead that it knocked him unconscious and temporarily disorientated the others.

Now Bunny appeared and aimed a small knife hilt first at the boss's stomach. He responded by smiling and not even trying to dodge, doubtless thinking, 'This daft creature doesn't know which way round to throw a knife!' Certainly, what hit his tubby paunch was a very bulbous, rubbery hilt, and he barely felt it. However, he very soon changed from smirking silence to howling agony: the knife so bounced, at about 90°, *as the rabbit had planned,* that its sharp point now transfixed the man's foot.

Buster was still nursing his hand from his abortive attempt to penetrate the door a moment before Jim succeeded. With his other hand, however, he thumped Pasty-Face so hard that the crook now looked like a vampire's victim. Red-and-tubby Face now panicked, tried to shoot Buster and missed, then ran towards the doorway. Keeper felled him with a carefully aimed throw of the ashtray.

"Smoking can be dangerous," commented Bunny.

Quickly gathering files, CDs, and external hard drives, the victorious friends now left the building and hurried to a wider, busier, and more salubrious street to find a bus, taxi, or subway train. The last option proved the easiest, and with a map of Sydney, they headed to where Buster had left the spaceship.

As they travelled, Keeper texted Nature: 'Mission done. Now meet at the Royal Botanic Gardens (near the Opera House) for a quick lift home.'

Then he turned to Buster: "I trust the spaceship will be clearly visible from any point in the gardens?"

Buster nodded.

Keeper continued: "What was your earlier howl of agony about?"

Buster grimaced ruefully, nursing his swollen hand. "Monkey sent us your coordinates, urging us to hurry, as you might be walking into more trouble than you could cope with. To save time, I thumped the first and then the second door open, thinking I had discovered my power-packed punch. But they were of flimsy chipboard construction. When I tried the last, unexpectedly solid door, I believe I lost my power-packed punch."

"OK – I'll try not to laugh. And I'm very grateful you all turned up when you did."

"By the way," replied the young astronaut, "Monkey himself went to give Nature any needed backup."

Chapter 22

GOING HOME

The late afternoon sun was reflected on the spaceship, where it was moored in the middle of the Botanic Gardens. Families of tourists and residents were crowding around. Buster saw his mate, Whiskey, standing on the lawn under the pilot door.

"Guided tour for twenty Ozzie dollars," said the cheeky dog.

Buster had to laugh. "I'm sure you've made a fast buck in my absence," he said, "but we're moving as soon as our last two passengers arrive."

"Uh, who's that?"

"Nature and Monkey," put in Keeper, "and I think I can see them now – at the end of that long path beyond the hothouse and those tall palms. Do you see?"

"I think you're right," said Buster: "So the rest of you get on board, and, Whiskey, be useful and start up the engines."

"Aye aye, Capt'n!"

The dog scampered up the metal ladder and moved to the cockpit. A whirring sound began, gradually getting faster.

Keeper waved at Nature, and she returned the salute as she and Monkey approached. Amidst some claps and cheers, they joined those already on board.

Slowly and majestically, the spacecraft rose into the amber sky, then turned westward with boosted velocity. Keeper and Nature held hands, both so thankful that their perilous adventure was now over.

"What if the Sydney authorities go back on their promises?" asked Nature.

"Then we'll go independent," replied Keeper, looking determined.

Jim chatted to Buster as they travelled.

"Do you have a name for this spaceship?"

"Yes – it's painted on the starboard side – Anastasia II, so named after the comic character Dan Dare's craft: it means 'rising upwards' in Greek."

"All Greek to me … but what brought you to our neck of the woods?"

"I have two younger brothers who live in or around Barleybag – your military leader, Steemer, and one of your chief pilots, Digger. They share my surname, Hawkins. I was hoping to meet up with them and maybe get a job in the same area. We also have a cousin, Flash, who, I am led to believe, runs a small navy somewhere opposite Kangaroo Island."

"Crumbs!" Jim's eyes lit up. "We'd love it, I reckon, if you settled in our community. Judging by the great help you've already given us, we'd be daft not to offer you a job and a place to live."

"Splendid! Well, we're over Barleybag now; so where would be the best place to land?"

"Better ask Keeper: he's the boss."

On Keeper's instructions, Buster carefully brought the spaceship down on The Rind, a smooth, grassy recreational patch near the harbour.

KEEPER
TARGAH
(OR TARZAN)
HECTOR
BUSTER
"ACHILLES" OR
"STEEMER"
"PERSEUS, OR
"DIGGER"

Chapter 23

MEANWHILE - BACK AT THE BURROW

It had been noticed by three sneaky witches that Bunny had left his burrow and not returned after at least five hours. This, they thought, was a big chance to invade and destroy.

Sometimes they needed to duck their heads, but Bunny had designed the tunnels to accommodate and welcome friends; so on the whole the witches proceeded confidently into his home. What they didn't know was that a hidden CCTV had triggered their arrival. As they turned a sharp corner, they saw, lit up by the walled fairy lights, a particularly small, vacant-looking rabbit (it was, in fact, our friend Boo) and what might have been a small hare, this last animal bouncing on its feet as if skipping, except with no rope.

"Heh, heh!" gloated the leading witch, clearly intending to spiflicate the sickeningly sweet and innocent-looking creatures with effortless ease.

But like the famous Philistine, he fatally misjudged the opposition. There was a high swishing sound, and Bouncy (the hare, genetically modified squirrel, or whatever it was) whirled a slingshot straight at his throat so that he fell, gasping, to the tunnel floor.

The other two witches looked down in stunned surprise. Then one felt a slight bop on the ear: Boo was perched on the near-high ledge. As the witch cursed and tried to dislodge him, he jumped over to the shield rim of the other intruder, ducked behind it, and then somehow appeared on the villain's shoulder.

"I'll get the annoying brat!" yelled the first witch.

He lunged forward. His companion, however, who had also just now been bopped, moved to catch the impudent rabbit and instead caught the full force of his fellow witch in a crunching collision that the little tormenting pest had – as they realized too late - cunningly engineered.

Picking themselves up and cursing solidly, the two would-be homewreckers now hurried after Boo and Bouncy.

"There they are!" hissed the one witch to the other.

The silhouettes of the two animals appeared on a rocky ledge, which was set above a yawning deep gorge.

"Hey, hey!" the witch gloatingly whispered: "we'll rush at them and knock them over the edge. Ready? ... NOW!"

Sure enough, in a matter of seconds, two helpless bodies were hurtling down to an almost certain death or the worst headaches ever imagined.

The two figures left above looked down with smug satisfaction.

"Lucky we sidestepped," said Bouncy.

Chapter 24

KEEPER'S PROPOSAL

It was a beautiful late Spring day. The pink and white blossoms resembled confetti from a distance and sweet popcorn close up. Most of the trees were partly dressed in lime green, vying with the grass verges in sunlit brightness, especially where pearls of moisture enhanced the shimmering hues.

Nature's heart was a flutter as she nourished a fair guess as to what would make this walk and this day so special. It was now about five years since Keeper had danced with her at Monkey's party, and exactly two weeks since they had rescued the prospector, Bruce, from the Rangers and witches.

Keeper held her hand with gentle pressure, indicating how much he valued her constant warmth. They passed the harbour entrance and the red brick lift bridge opposite. Now, the footpath led up onto the Downs.

"Can I read you a poem?" asked Keeper.

Nature nodded. "Yes, I'd like to hear it."

He took a piece of paper from his pocket, unfolded it and read:

No one floats my boat like you.

All about you makes me glad.

Tell me that you love me true.

Until then, I shall be sad.

Reassure me you are mine.

Every day, and we'll be fine.

Love me till the end of time;

Always haunt me when I dream;

Never leave me all alone.

Girl, we make a winning team.

There's no mountain we can't climb,

Over problems reign supreme:

Nothing spoils our peace sublime.

"It seems that I am your Muse," laughed Nature: "know what I mean?"

"It was an acrostic," said Keeper. "By the way, how are your two dogs?"

"Summer's looking after them today. I think she'd planned to walk them through Targah's Forest."

"She and Targah get on well together." Keeper sounded wistful.

"I've been meaning to ask you ever since you freed me from Spawn's clutches… "

"Go on."

"What was in that note you passed him? – or her: the gender is not obvious."

"I agree. Ducky thinks Spawn is, like most witches, female; my guess is male. Ted, the would-be private eye, and Scottie, the budding biologist, found two Z chromosomes in some witch casualties. Perhaps they're all sexless – unlike us," he added with a wicked smile.

Nature gave him a searching coffee-dark look: "And what about the note?"

"Oh, yes. It said that I, the hunchback, had saved his life by making him let you go. I wrote that you had a hidden biological weapon that would destroy not only yourself but anyone within six metres of range, and I told him I'd incapacitated some of our rifles. You never know:

the clumsy 'hunchback' may be able to do more useful work as a double agent!"

As Keeper spoke, he caught sight of a bulbous-eyed, garishly dressed gypsy woman, who seemed to be beckoning him.

"Stay here just a minute," he told Nature. "I'll just go over and see what she wants. I think I recognise her. It's Mrs. Polo from Malt Lake."

The old woman had a tray of relatively cheap jewellery.

"Something for your sweetheart?" she wheedled: "a brooch perhaps? Look at this one: it's beautiful."

She held out an imitation amethyst sample.

"See, the pin moves in and out of place quite easily."

She demonstrated, then suddenly used it to stab Keeper's extended palm.

Nature heard his cry of agony and ran forward.

The nasty hag ran off, howling with triumph: "Now I'll get Spawn's reward!"

Nature knelt by the slumped Keeper.

There was the suggestion of a tear in his eye.

"I've screwed up," he whispered, "and I wanted this day to be so happy."

"I won't let you die."

"Easy to say, but you don't know their poisons. Oh, nothing ever hurt like this."

Nature reached into her handbag and produced a tiny flask and three green tablets.

"Quick, swill the tablets down with this." She uncorked the liquid and dropped the lot into his mouth.

It tasted foul, but Keeper suddenly felt his vital forces returning.

"How on earth…?" he began.

"You'd be surprised what I learned while I was in captivity, especially as to my captors' favourite poisons. And I guessed when I saw that last look of utter hatred on Spawn's face that he would try to get back at us. You were the most likely target, and I've kept this antidote with me constantly."

"You are wonderful," said Keeper. "I want to give you my most fragrant deep red roses, yet the perfect rose will always be you. And I'm so grateful for the antidote but jealous of it too."

"What do you mean?"

"You said you keep it with you constantly. That's where I want to be – always with you."

"Sharing all the danger?"

"No. You saved me today. I want to keep you from danger in the future."

"Wow! My knight in shining armour! Look out. I may prove very demanding."

"Well, I'll do my very best to look after you and keep you happy," he promised.

Then the 'perfect rose' turned a deep red herself as she saw Keeper open the little box that contained the prospector's ring.

The warm afternoon sunlight glimmered through the salmon-coloured, purple-edged clouds on the far horizon; two magpies foraged the grass; a snow-white screaming seagull divided the sky, and out to sea little boats and distant liners moved onward in the prospect of grand future adventures.

"We'll get you next time!"

WHAT HAS THE BOOK TO OFFER?

This story is a romantic fantasy. It's sheer escapism for all who are young at heart. But it's also a story with humans and talking animals, following the popular, winning combination in previous books and films, such as Anchors Aweigh, The Wizard of Oz, Winnie the Pooh, Bedknobs and Broomsticks and Paddington. There are witches (always bad!), genies: in all, a host of memorable characters, with exotic settings and realistic make-believe and nail-biting, cliff-hanging moments. Just read the first chapter… and I think you'll be hooked. You are in a new world.

www.ingramcontent.com/pod-product-compliance
Lightning Source LLC
Chambersburg PA
CBHW041413010726
47507CB00005B/258